Under A Christmas Moon

A SMALL-TOWN HOLIDAY ROMANCE

AN ELF HOLLOW ROMANCE
BOOK ONE

SAVANNAH FORD

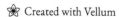

To my family for all the love, support and encouragement over the years.
To my tribe who encouraged me to take this step. I wouldn't be here without you!
For Martin, for giving me the opportunity to follow my dreams. And for showing me what a real hero looks like!

Chapter One

Quinn McAllister picked her way through the icy, salt-covered sidewalks of Elf Hollow, Minnesota. Snowflakes, caught in a whirlwind, danced around her head and sparkled like mini gems in the pre-dawn sky. Niko, her eleven-month-old Alaskan Malamute, caught a scent and came to an abrupt halt, muzzle deep in a snow pile.

Sinking into her coat, she gazed around the quaint town. The barest hint of deep coral touched the horizon turning everything a soft blush, and for an instant, she stood inside a child's snow globe.

Alone. Frozen in time.

A place of peace, free of doubt and worry. A precious blink of solace. And then the sun broke the line between earth and sky and the moment was gone.

The mantle of reality draped around her shoulders. Her hand curled around the legal notice she'd received from Henrietta's attorney the day before. Somehow, she'd have to find a way to break the news to everyone.

A gentle tug on Niko's leash got his attention, and they resumed their morning trek. The crunch beneath her boots echoed in the hush of freshly fallen snow. An arctic gust drove into her as she turned the corner. She pulled the hood tighter around her face and shoved her gloved hands back in the fur-lined pockets.

This was her favorite time of day. Without the barrage of cars headed to the ski lodge, she could think without the chaos of life.

Ignoring the *Closed* sign, Quinn ducked into the Land's End Diner and stomped the slush off her boots. Pine from the freshly scrubbed floors burned the tiny hairs in her nose and pushed the clean, frigid scent of winter to a memory.

She locked the door, tucked the gloves into her coat pockets, and hung it up. Tinseled garland twined with colorful Christmas lights draped from the ceiling. The plate-glass window, announcing Land's End Diner, boasted a freshly painted Christmas scene complete with tree and packages. Mistletoe already hung from every light, and holiday music blasted from the speakers. She loved this time of year. Maybe because the couple that raised her, Emerson and Henrietta— Henri for short—Wagner, loved it so much they built an entire business around it.

"Hello?" She waved Niko to his rug in the corner and smiled as he plopped down, crossed his paws, and gave her a puppy smile. He'd been a gift from Henrietta last Christmas. She didn't like the idea of Quinn on walks around town in the dark, so Henrietta bought her a protector. The problem was, the overgrown puppy was more troublemaker than guardian.

The scent of bacon made her stomach rumble and reminded her she hadn't eaten a good meal in weeks. "Where is everyone?"

As she approached the counter, her gaze landed on the glow of an unattended candle, and she stiffened. Sweat beaded her upper lip, and she choked on fear like a fist down her throat. For an instant, a ghosted image of her thirteen-year-old self, surrounded by smoke and flames, flickered before her.

Niko's warm body appeared by her side and pressed against her thigh, a solid presence that kept her from becoming a pile of useless bones on the floor. Her fingers curled in the comfort of his thick fur as the bang of pots and pans jarred her from the trance of fear.

The kitchen door swung open, and the smiling face of the diner's manager and her best friend, Amy Collins, emerged. "She's here," Amy shouted over her shoulder, her voice tinged with excitement. As she moved further into the room, her smile faded to confusion. Then her gaze fell on the candle. "I'm sorry, sweetie, you're early." She blew out the flame as she passed the counter and continued on her way.

Quinn drew in a long, steady breath and willed her heart rate from a heavy metal drum solo to a slow tango. When would she get over this silly fear? A candle for heaven's sake.

"Come here, you big, beautiful ball of fur." Amy patted her leg and dropped to her knee by Niko's rug with a bowl of water in hand.

Niko turned his gaze to Quinn and waited for her release before he trotted to Amy, tail wagging.

Quinn's mouth quivered with a shadow of a smile as her best friend made goo-goo noises at Niko and whispered sweet nothings into his fur.

Inseparable since sixth grade, Amy and Quinn were as opposite as two people could get, the Yin and Yang, the light and dark, the peanut butter and jelly.

"How was your walk down?"

"Cold." Quinn suppressed a shiver as she poured a mug of coffee. She lowered her lids and cupped her frozen fingers around the warmth and inhaled. Nothing like the aroma of coffee beans to spark the brain and cleanse the oily feel of fear. "But quiet. Just the way I like it."

She smiled at Amy and joined her at the table. The third party of their Friday morning group came from the kitchen with a tray of eggs, bacon, and toast, along with a treat for Niko.

"Good morning, sunshine." Carole Ann put the food down and wrapped Quinn in a bear hug. The last of her three kids had left for college in the fall, leaving her with an empty nest. That meant all the bottled-up motherly love fell on Quinn and Amy. "We've missed you." She took a seat and passed their plates.

Quinn reached for a piece of toast and suppressed a soft laugh. "I saw you yesterday."

"Yes, but we haven't met for breakfast since..." Carole Ann's voiced faded, and her fingers fiddled with a napkin. "In weeks."

The covert exchange between the two women didn't go unnoticed by Quinn. She paused toast halfway to her mouth. A vague sense of dread flowed through her veins. She knew the look all too well. Everyone in town gave her the same glassy-eyed stare of pity. The tenuous hold on her composure slipped like shifting sand, reminding her of what she'd lost and the uncertainty of her future.

Carole Ann patted her hand. "I'm sorry, honey, I didn't mean to bring that up."

"Yeah, let's eat. I'm starved," Amy chimed in.

Quinn dropped the toast on her plate and wiped her hands on the napkin. "Don't do that."

"Do what?" Amy and Carole Ann asked in unison.

"This." Quinn waved her hands between them. "I'm not a piece of Henri's old china. You don't need to insulate me in bubble wrap. I'm a big girl. Let's... put it out there. Henrietta is gone, and she won't be back and..." A sob choked off anything more.

How could Henri be gone? The only family Quinn had, Henrietta and her husband Emerson, both gone.

Alone. Again.

She blinked away the tears pooling at her lash line. "I'm fine. I need to figure out what happens next."

Silence settled around them like an old itchy blanket. Weighted. Awkward.

"I'm going to say it." Carole Ann broke the silence. "You wipe your tears, and you carry on. You have a business to run. We need to start making plans for the holidays. The retirement home already contacted me about their party. You can't afford to sit around too timid to move forward."

The words pierced her vulnerable psyche, but Quinn needed to hear them.

"I don't mean to be heartless," Carole Ann continued. "You know how much I loved Henrietta, but she wouldn't want you to wallow in grief and self-pity. You're stronger than that. Too many people depend on you to carry us through the holidays. There will be time enough for grieving when the season is over."

Quinn couldn't argue with the logic. Christmas was the busiest time of year for everyone in Elf Hollow with reservations at the B&B booked a year in advance. Henri's birthday was on Christmas Eve, and she and Emerson celebrated their anniversary in December. All three of their businesses stemmed from their love of the season.

From the day after Thanksgiving until the end of January, the entire town went into holiday mode. Decorations had been up for days, and all the party plans fell to the Wagners, now her. She couldn't, *wouldn't* let everybody down. Her hand curled around the wad of paper she'd shoved in her pocket before leaving the house.

She'd wanted to tell them about the letter from Henri's attorney. Needed to tell them. But she didn't have the heart.

Not yet. Not until she found out what was going on. Henri and Emerson were like parents to her. In her mind, she knew they wouldn't leave her out in the cold. But this letter opened up too many questions. And she didn't have any answers.

Amy retrieved her laptop, and they proceeded with their usual Friday morning agenda. For the next forty-five minutes, they lost themselves in planning the week ahead. Guests didn't start arriving at the B&B for another seven days, this would be prep week. As the General Manager of all the properties in the Wagner's Trust, Quinn oversaw the diner, the Christmas Shoppe, and the B&B, but her three managers handled the day-to-day. Amy managed the restaurant with Carole Ann in charge of the kitchen, and Jim Lovette ran the shop, leaving the B&B in Quinn's hands.

Quinn twirled her fork. The flash of silver caught the light from above and held her spellbound.

"Hello? Where did you go?" Amy flicked Quinn's ear. "Did you hear anything I said?"

"What?" Quinn shook her head. "No, I mean yes, something about a list..."

Amy laughed and stood to pile their plates on the tray. "Do you want me to start a list of what we need for cookie baking?"

"Yes, of course."

Carole Ann rose to follow Amy to the back. "The boys should be arriving anytime for the breakfast shift. I need to get back there and start the prep."

"Wait," Quinn said. "Can I ask you something?"

"Anything."

"You've known... knew Henrietta for a long time, right?"

"Yes, she and my mother were friends. Why?"

"Did she ever mention any family? A brother or sister?"

"You and Emerson are the only family she ever talked about." Carole Ann cocked her head with a curious gaze.

6

"Why do you ask?"

Quinn opened her mouth and then closed it without a word. She had no clue what to say. Her thoughts scattered like ants pouring from a disrupted anthill. She shook her head and stood. "No reason. I feel like I didn't know Henri as well as I thought." She grabbed her coat and headed for the door. "Tell Amy I said goodbye. I'll be at the B&B if you need me." She patted her leg for Niko.

Back at the B&B, she went in search of the teenager she hired part-time to clean. "Kaylee, can you get the Lakeside and Aurora rooms made up, please?"

The eighteen-year-old pranced into the foyer from the bathroom. "I didn't know we had guests." Kaylee dropped the bucket of cleaning supplies on the counter and tightened her strawberry blonde ponytail.

"They'll be here late this afternoon or early evening. Have them all set up." Quinn followed Niko to the office and shut the door before she pulled the crumpled letter from her pocket. Niko laid his ball at her feet and waited for her to play their favorite game of fetch. She gave the toy a half-hearted kick across the room and focused on the paper.

Dear Ms. McAllister,

I'm writing to inform you of the reading of Henrietta Wagner's Last Will and Testament that will take place Monday, December 3rd. Mrs. Wagner's nephews will be arriving on Friday, November 30th. Please have rooms ready for their arrival...

The letter went on to provide instructions for their arrival and the details of the appointment. She dropped into the chair and tossed the message on her desk. In all the years she lived with them, Henrietta never mentioned any family. Who were these mystery nephews, and what did they mean for the future of Elf Hollow?

Chapter Two

"Really, Joe? It's been almost three full hours since you called to tell me what a screw up I am. I think that's a record." The use of his father's first name was like tossing a hand grenade into a gasoline can, guaranteed to cause white-hot rage. Ash Larsen shrugged it away. He'd given up years ago trying to please the old man. More fun to poke the bear. Nothing Joe Larsen's youngest son did would ever be good enough.

"What a... I... disrespectful..." Angry words sputtered from the man with whom Ash had the misfortune of sharing DNA.

Ash jammed his free hand on the ceiling of the banana yellow VW bug as Chandra, his current fling, took the speed bump too fast. "Watch the thing. The thing — It's not racing season, and you're not Danica Patrick!"

"What'd you say to me, boy?" A now composed voice of ice-cold venom slithered through the phone line.

"Wasn't talking to you, Dad. Seriously, you're going to kill someone," Ash snapped. The poor guy about to step off the curb threw them a scowl as he fell over his luggage in his haste to save his life.

"Boy, you are crossing the line. You're supposed to meet your brother at the airport, and you're out messing around."

Ash swallowed the sharp taste of yearning. His father would always think the worst of him. Just once he wished some of that fatherly love and concern would spill over onto him. "No worries, Dad. Eric is a big boy. He'll survive." One last speedway maneuver and the car slammed to a stop half on, half off the curb. He had no idea how they'd gotten to the Houston airport in one piece.

"I still don't see why I can't go," Chandra grumbled.

"Who is that? That graphic artist, tattooed from head to toe?" His father asked. "Dammit, Ash, you had one thing to do today, get to the airport and fly out—"

"That's two things. Sorry, Dad. Gotta go. Wouldn't want to keep big bro waiting." He disconnected and tossed the phone in the pocket of his duffel bag. He would pay for that later.

Chandra adjusted the rearview mirror and applied another coat of cherry red lipstick. "Come on, sugar, you know we'll have a good time."

He wiped a hand over his face. This trip couldn't have come at a better time. He opened the door and tossed his bag on the ground before he untangled himself from the cramped tin can that passed for a car.

This *relationship,* as some would define it, should've ended seven days ago. He had one hard and fast rule, no hookups over three weeks. *Ever.* Except for this time.

He didn't even have a good reason. He suppressed a grunt of laughter. Of course, it could have something to do with his father's reaction when Ash showed up at the birthday party with Chandra in tow. Sleeve tattoos from shoulder to wrists, eyebrow rings, and her less-than-refined personality almost gave the old man a coronary on his big day. What other justification did he need?

Besides, he couldn't break it off with her, not with Christmas a few weeks away. No one should spend the holidays alone. Despite rumors, he didn't have a heart of stone. If the week-long absence brought it to its natural conclusion, all the better.

Ash picked up his bag and turned, ready to make his goodbyes. Instead, he collided with his girl of the moment as she planted her feet squarely in front of him. Hands on curvy hips, she tilted her head to gaze up at him. Long legs, tanned from days in the Texas sun, ran from cowboy boots to a scrap of material that posed as a skirt. Her barely-there tee shirt boasted a black Christmas tree adorned with white skulls, and the words *kill me under the mistletoe* scrolled around the image. Her design. Bold, brash, sexy.

"Look at you, all spicy, hot..." Ash waved his hands. "And not in the car." He didn't want to hurt her any more than the other women who passed through the revolving door of his life. He didn't blame them; he wouldn't know a good relationship if it jumped up and bit him in the butt. After all, he had a reputation as a playboy to uphold.

Squeezing her shoulder, he planted a quick peck on her cheek and moved to make his escape. "I'll be back before you know it."

Her lips pressed into a straight line, and she crossed her arms over her chest. Her foot tapped out an angry staccato on the pavement. "You promised we would do something fun. I canceled my plans and everything."

"Aw, angel, don't be that way. I didn't plan on my aunt dying." *Or the need to settle her estate.* He glanced at his watch and heaved a sigh of frustration. He had enough confrontation in his life he didn't need anymore. He forced a smile. "I'll be back in a few days, and we'll talk."

She twined her arms around his neck and pressed her body against his. "I won't bother you. You won't know I'm there. What do ya say, sugar? You. Me. Ski slopes at Christmas?"

He gave her credit. She was as persistent as a bag full of rattlesnakes seeking an exit. But he knew better. This had nothing to do with his charming personality and clever wit. They never stayed for him. *He* might not have a bankroll, but his family did. The women stayed for all the perks that came along with being a *Larsen*. Social status, parties, and good times. Nothing more.

"Fine. If I can't go, you should at least pay for my gas out here. Not like it's down the street." She pouted.

Liberating himself from the tangle of limbs, he reached for his wallet and pulled out a hundred-dollar bill. "All I have is a C-note."

She hesitated, and in that split second, a tendril of hope curled through him. Hope that maybe someone wanted him more than all the other stuff.

Then, like all the rest, she grabbed the cash. "I'll see you in a few days." Sparing him nothing more than a quick air kiss, she escaped to the driver's side and disappeared.

Ash waved above his head as he did an about-face and headed into the airport, a sigh of relief on his lips. One day he needed to re-evaluate his life choices.

He emerged from the revolving door into the industrial style terminal of Houston Intercontinental Airport. The obnoxious blare of Christmas music blasted from overhead speakers. The familiar aromas of perfume, sweat, cleaning products, and coffee greeted him in an offensive combination that reminded him how much he hated to travel during the holidays.

His brother, Eric, stepped from the shadows. "Booty-call stash, or do we need to find an ATM?"

"Dude, what's the matter with you?" Ash bit the inside of

his cheek hard enough that blood dotted his tongue. "You don't jump out of the shadows at someone. You're lucky I didn't deck you."

"Good to see you, too." Eric nodded at the door. "Isn't that the woman from dad's birthday party?"

"Yup." Ash swung his bag over his back and fell in step with his brother. Taking a deep breath through his nose, he exhaled, twisted his head from side to side, and willed his back muscles to release.

Eric snorted. "That was over a month ago. You expect me to believe you've finally decided to commit to a long-term relationship?"

"Really? That's how this is going to go? I haven't seen you in two weeks, and you're going to give me a hard time about my love life?" His blood pressure threatened to blow through the top of his head like champagne exploding from a bottle. When Ash was still in high school, his father declared open season on his relationships. To this day, he still took every opportunity to taunt him about his lack of commitment. Eric used to be an ally, but all that changed once he brought home the perfect wife to make dad proud.

Ash choked down anything more he had to say. It had all been hashed out many times before. Nothing changed. *You don't care. You don't care.* He repeated his mantra several times before he continued. "By the time I get back from this trip, I'll be a distant memory. A blip in her life."

"Doesn't it ever get old?"

Ash opened his mouth but stopped short of a response. Instead, he pressed his lips into a tight slash. He turned his attention to his driver's license as they neared the checkpoint.

"You're thirty years old." Eric reminded him. "Don't you think it's time to settle down and enjoy the next phase in life?"

The TSA agent checked the boarding pass and handed it back to Ash.

"And who is the judge of what *the next stage in life* is? You? Dad? No thanks, I'm good." He clenched his jaw until a muscle jumped beneath his ear, and a rush of heat flushed through his veins. He didn't know why he let Eric get on his nerves. After all these years, his skin should be as leathery and impervious as an alligator's hide.

"How about Gran? She's the one who tied up your trust fund until you got married."

Mounting frustration made Ash's movements short and jerky as he tossed his duffel bag on the conveyer belt.

It had been a year, and still, he didn't understand why Gran did that to him. She knew his father would never forgive him for taking his first breath at the same time his mother breathed her last. It was a shadow he lived under every day of his life. After years of humiliation and loneliness, that money could've freed him from the bastard. She also knew Ash would never marry for anything less than love. Something he didn't believe existed.

"Brother, don't make this hard. Pick one of your gorgeous women and marry her. Dad will be happy, the woman thrilled, and your problems solved." Eric nudged his shoulder and then picked up his stuff to head for the gate.

Easier said than done. He wasn't cut out for marriage. And Eric knew that.

His brother lived a charmed life. Perfect wife, perfect kids, and he sat on the brink of being the next President of Cayman Oil. A perfect mini-me for their father. While Ash worked as the middleman in the Human Resource Department for all the oilfield workers, a job that sent him out in the field so much, he spent more time in hotels than his condo.

Eric pulled out his phone and got lost in an email. Ash took the time to regroup.

The two of them had always been close as kids, despite his

father doing his best to push them apart. But over the last few years, Eric became more and more like the old man.

They stepped off the moving walkway. An older gentleman in a wheelchair worked to retrieve a book that had fallen out of his bag but landed out of his reach. Three people had the nerve to glance at his efforts as they made a wide berth to avoid helping. Ash groaned as he made his way over to the book.

"Here you go. Do you need help getting to your gate?"

"Thank you. No. I'm right here." The old guy gestured in a vague wave to his right. "They parked me over in the corner and left me, but I decided to find something to read for the plane. I better get back before I'm missed." He settled the book in his lap and wheeled himself to the gate.

Ash joined Eric at their gate, taking the bench seat next to him. Two young boys shouted their Christmas lists at each other as they ran around tripping over bags and stepping on toes while their parents stared at phones.

Ash sighed. It would be a full flight, packed in like cattle headed to market. He felt sorry for whoever sat near that young family. "What did you find out about the inheritance?"

"It's three businesses. A Bed and Breakfast, a Christmas shop, and a diner in Elf Hollow, Minnesota. Once we land in Minneapolis, we'll rent a car and make the four-hour drive. I'm told someone by the name of Quinn McAllister will meet us and fill us in."

"What do we know about McAllister?"

Eric flipped through the notes on his phone and shrugged. "Nothing other than that's our contact."

This potential windfall couldn't have come at a better time. Ash had a lead on the perfect rental location for his dream restaurant, but he needed first and last month's rent by the middle of the month. That he could cover, but restaurant start-ups weren't cheap. Working capital, reserves, insurance, living expenses until it became profitable. He needed a loan to make it all happen.

Three banks had turned him away, all citing his lack of experience and minimal assets. While he'd earned his culinary degree, he'd done nothing with it in ten years. It had been a way to get under his father's skin. And it turned into a way to express himself. He loved the joy his food brought to others.

His nest egg would only go so far. "Any idea what it's all worth?" Ash voiced what they were both thinking.

"I have my assistant working on it, but right now, I have no idea,"

He hadn't wished for his great-aunt's death. They didn't know she'd existed until two weeks ago when the letter from an attorney showed up, offered condolences, and stated he and Eric shared in her inheritance. This could be his last chance. It was either this or subjecting some unsuspecting woman to a loveless marriage to claim his trust fund. He didn't think he could sink that low.

Their conversation died off until they were in the air. They were seated in first-class, and he'd been arrogant enough to assume the happy Christmas family would be in economy. Guess fate was having a laugh at him as they sat behind him. Every few minutes, the back of his seat took a hit. The raucous voices belted out the same childish Christmas tune over and over until the words pounded in his head. He hated December with all its joyous prattle and commercialism.

"What do you think happened?" Ash gave up trying to read the in-flight magazine. "Between Gran and her sister."

Eric shook his head. "I have no clue. Dad didn't even know Gran had a sister."

"Do you think Granddad knew?"

"According to the report our in-house investigator gave me, Sadie and her twin Henrietta were born in St. Paul, Minnesota, nineteen thirty-nine. Sadie married Travis Larsen in Houston in nineteen fifty-nine. Henrietta married Emerson Wagner in nineteen seventy-three."

"Okay, Granddad—"

"Wait, there's more. Travis Larsen, born in St. Paul, Minnesota, nineteen thirty-nine disappeared from any records in Minnesota and showed up in Houston." Eric flipped off his phone and slipped it in his shirt pocket. "Looks like Gran and Grandpa left Minneapolis for Houston and never looked back."

Ash peered out the window and tried to imagine what tragic event could have run his grandparents out of Minnesota because he knew his grandmother. It would take a god-awful incident to make her turn her back on family.

Chapter Three

O f all the dumb luck. "Niko, no! Stand down. Off!" Quinn shouted all the command words they'd learned in obedience school, but his thunderous howls rose another two octaves on the baritone scale as the squirrel hopped over Niko's head and scampered across the top of the counter.

Quinn shoved her hands in a couple of oven mitts and grabbed an empty pot from the stove. Carole Ann would kill her if she knew what she was about to do. But desperate times and all. She needed something to contain the rodent. "Niko, no!" The box of Christmas decorations she'd carried from the attic crashed to the floor, dumping the squirrel's wad of nesting material along with a box of now-smashed glass ornaments.

The overgrown puppy tried to stop his headlong charge, but his feet couldn't get traction on the hardwood, and he slid through the swinging door into the dining room. The squirrel ran between his legs into the open area of the house.

Blast! At least in the kitchen, it couldn't go anywhere else.

She'd had a plan. A good, solid plan. She liked plans. She had three planners, lovingly put together with washi-tape,

17

color-coded pens, and used every day. Decorating. *That* was the plan. Nowhere on any of the books did it say *chase squirrel through house*. But then who anticipated a squirrel hibernating in a box of Christmas decorations?

She glanced at the wall clock. Almost nine p.m. Henrietta's nephews were due, and she still had half her to-do list left. A crash from the dining room reminded her she had bigger problems than an unfinished checklist. Not the first impression she hoped to make.

With a renewed sense of urgency, she dropped to her knees and exited the kitchen, pot in hand, on the hunt for the fuzzy-tailed menace.

"You graduated number one in your obedience class," she grumbled. "If Bryce finds out he is going to come take your ribbon," she yelled at the absent Niko.

Another crash followed by a yelp came from the lobby area. Quinn shuffled to her feet and hurried in the direction of the noise. Niko's bark reached hysterical levels. A sign of either victory or frustration.

As she rounded the corner to the lobby, she thought she heard the low mumble of voices, but the ringing in her ears drowned out anything coherent. The image of a man standing in the open doorway, however, hand poised above the handle, couldn't be mistaken. The squirrel smelled freedom and made a run for it, Niko right behind him. Panic seized her. If Niko got out, she had no idea how far he would run or if he'd come back. He'd never been out without her.

"Shut the door! Don't let him out," she hollered as she turned the last corner and collided with a solid, warm body. The door slammed shut at the same time Niko ran headlong into it. Quinn hit the floor hard enough she bit her tongue and dropped the pot.

After almost twenty minutes of yelling, barking, and rodent squeaks, the silence, so pristine it took on a life of its own, echoed in the room. As her vision cleared, a pair of jean-clad legs appeared directly in front of her.

A hand came into view and long, tanned fingers curled around the pot before he handed it to her. "I hope that wasn't dinner," said a smooth, masculine voice with a hint of laughter.

Heat flushed up her neck, bloomed across her face before spreading to her ears. She knew from past experience the tight, itchy skin glowed like a neon sign. She squeezed her lids tight, wished with all her might to be transported somewhere else. Anywhere but there.

The weight of Niko's hundred-pound body plopped next to her, and his wet tongue bathed her cheek in slow, slobbery kisses.

And there it was. Total humiliation.

Legs squatted, and an oval face with five o'clock shadow along a softly squared jaw came into view. *Holy, wowza, baby!* What a face.

Her tongue flicked across parched lips, and she repeatedly swallowed, desperate for moisture in a mouth dry as dust. One day when she retold this story, and she had no doubt it would be retold many times, what would she remember most? The light brown eyes with golden flecks filled with mischief, or the wide cocky grin that flashed a sexy dimple and even, white teeth.

"Is this a bad time?" This man exuded trouble. He reached his arm in front of her and let Niko sniff his hand before he scratched the dog behind the ear.

Her heart hammered against her ribs, and her jaw went slack. Words, as elusive as butterflies, fled in the presence of her current situation.

Another pair of legs came into sight. "Quit playing around, Ash. We're looking for Quinn McAllister."

The one called Ash stood up, and each man grabbed an arm to help her to her feet.

She cleared her throat and tried to gain composure. "That would be me." She nudged Niko to the side and pulled off the oven mitts.

"You're Quinn McAllister?" The other man, shorter and blonder, had the same brown eyes absent the golden flecks.

She brushed the seat of her pants and wiped her hands. "You were expecting someone else?" She had no idea why his question prickled, but it did.

"My brother meant no offense, but we were expecting someone... older." Ash's voice, a rich, deep rumble, vibrated to the bottom of her chest.

"*You* manage all Henrietta Wagner's holdings?" The other one asked.

The two guys couldn't be more annoying if they tried. "Yes. I'm the general manager of Wagner Holdings, and I run the B&B." Right after Emerson died, Henrietta added Quinn as the General Manager of all the holdings. Did that offer any protection for her and their employees? That remained to be seen. She made a mental note to ask the attorney when she talked to him. She sought the security of the lobby counter and put some professional distance between them.

"Can you tell us what's in the holdings?" The shorter one asked.

Yes, she could, but did she want to? "I'm sorry, you have me at a disadvantage. You apparently know all about me but, other than you being Henrietta's nephews, I have no idea who you are." She crossed her arms and clenched her jaw. "You are Henrietta's nephews, correct?" She pinned them both with as much intimidation as she could muster. No easy feat when they both stood almost a foot taller.

"Relax, Angel. My name is Ash Larsen, this surly dude is my brother, Eric. And I'm afraid whatever disadvantage there is would be mutual. Until a week ago neither of us even knew Henrietta existed." Ash gave her a smile meant to charm and manipulate.

Angel? Seriously, who fell for that? She knew his type. A playboy with a wicked smile and an ego larger than the room they stood in. And given her track record, if she weren't careful, it would be the heartbreak of Ty all over again. "Then we have something in common," Quinn said. "Until last week, no one here knew anything about any relatives. In fact, all we, I, know is you are Henri's nephews. I don't even know if she had a sister or a brother."

"Sister," Ash said. "Our grandmother."

"Did your grandmother tell you what happened between them?" Having some answers to the mystery would be nice.

"She died over a year ago and our grandfather a few years before," Ash said.

Eric sighed. "It's been a long day, Ms. McAllister. Could we possibly get our rooms and get settled? We could pick this conversation up over something to eat."

Quinn froze. Something to eat? How could she be so stupid? She'd been too worried about keeping their presence a secret from everyone in town she forgot to have Carole Ann send over food. No one even knew they were there. She spared a quick glance at her sports watch, too late to call the diner. They were already closing. "I'm afraid it's too late for dinner, I may be able to scrounge up some cheese and crackers and some grapes." She always kept easy meals around. The kind that didn't require the flame of a gas stove to cook.

The two men exchanged a questionable glance. "No offense, darlin', but this is a bed and breakfast, right?" Ash gave her a smile meant to charm her right out of her senses.

All the muscles in her face tightened. "Breakfast, being the operative word. It is after nine o'clock at night." Never mind she didn't tell Carole Ann to send up breakfast either. She'd deal with that issue in the morning.

She didn't miss the glance both men gave each other before they scanned the lobby.

"Curious. Where are all the guests? Are they in their rooms already?" Ash asked.

"We don't have any guests at the moment."

Eric turned his back and mumbled for Ash's ears only. "Not a good sign." His voice rose and fell in a sing-song tone.

"I can hear you." She plunked the wireless keyboard down on the counter. "For your information, we have plenty of guests. By this time next week, we'll be almost full. In fact, I had to put you in the rooms that share a bathroom."

"Shared bathroom? As in share with strangers?" Ash curled his lip. "You're joking."

"As a matter of fact, no. However, there are only two rooms that share, and I usually reserve those for people traveling as singles or if there is a large family that needs two rooms. I'm sure you'll survive."

"How many rooms do you have?" Eric asked.

"We have one on the main floor, four on the second, and the converted attic has three additional rooms." Quinn handed them their keys and led the way upstairs.

"And which one is yours?" Ash asked as they reached the top of the stairs.

"I don't have a room in the main house. I stay in the guest house at the back of the property. By the lake."

Eric stopped in the process of unlocking his door and spun around. "There's a guest house on the lake? How big is that? How close to the lake?" He turned to Ash, "Do you realize that could increase the value tremendously? The information provided didn't say anything about lakefront property."

"You need to make sure your secretary has that information when she contacts potential agents."

A chilling, tingling sensation raced across her scalp. Both men seemed to have forgotten about her. Doors opened, suitcases in hand, they stood jabbering about the potential increase in value to the real estate. AKA her home.

Her fingers flexed at her side. She may not have all the answers yet, but these two yahoos had another thing coming if they thought she would standby, twiddling her thumbs while they auctioned off Emerson and Henri's life's work.

"You can't seriously be thinking of selling." Her voice shrilled louder than she'd intended, and they both stared at her like she'd grown a pair of horns.

"Actually, the ski lodge has already expressed interest in the place," Eric said.

The ski lodge? They'd been trying to buy Henri out for years, and she refused out of principle. They wanted to tear it all down. Everything the Wagners spent a lifetime building would be gone.

"Tell me, Angel, what would you suggest we do?" Ash asked, his voice sweet and smooth like warm maple syrup on a cold winter morning.

She shivered, and her toes curled in her shoes. "I don't even like maple syrup."

"Excuse me?"

Did I say that out loud? Her hands flew to her face and willed the floor to open, to swallow her whole. "I... Don't. Call. Me. That." She gritted out from behind clenched teeth.

"What?" The confusion that clouded Ash's face would be comical if she weren't mortified.

"Would you look at that?" Eric chimed in. "A woman who is immune to Ash Larsen's charms. Ms. McAllister, it's been a real honor. Now, if you two will excuse me, I have a wife to call." He waved good night and disappeared into his room.

"You've called me that ridiculous name twice. Don't do it again." She glowered up at Ash before she marched off. It was late, and she was tired to the bone, but she needed to figure out her next move. Because no way could she allow them to sell Henri's legacy. Those two men didn't care a lick about Henri and Emerson or anything they'd built. All they cared about was the money. *Henri, I sure hope you knew what you were doing.*

Ash cocked his head. Steel rod at her back, movements mechanical. Annoyance etched in every line of her body.

None of it disguised her sweet curves.

He smiled, walked into his room, and shut the door behind him. Long hair that reminded him of caramel sauce on a sundae and eyes the prettiest blue. Almost navy. She was cute in a dignified, pit-bull-with a-bone kinda way.

Too bad her kind only wanted forever.

Chapter Four

Ash flipped the switch on the gas fireplace and crouched his towel-clad body as close to the blower as possible. He couldn't stop shivering or prevent the goosebumps from spreading across shower-damp skin. Ever since they left the comfort of the airport for the arctic air yesterday, he couldn't get warm. He'd slept under a pile of nightmare-inducing Christmas blankets, and he still woke up a Popsicle. As far as he was concerned, nobody should live like this. The cold seeped into his bones, freezing him from the inside. The only relief came from a hot shower which backfired as soon as he turned off the water.

God, what he wouldn't give for a blast of steamy-hot Houston air. He threw the towel on the bed and grabbed boxer briefs from the suitcase. He should have taken Eric's advice and bought long-johns. As he pulled on the warmth of jeans and a long-sleeved shirt, he cheered himself with one simple thought... only three days before they headed home.

He pulled on his snakebite resistant boots. Too bad his weren't winter resistant as well. He walked next door to Eric's room and banged on the door.

Eric opened it immediately and waved him in, pointing to the phone at his ear as he motioned for silence.

"Yes, sir, we have an appointment with the broker after the appointment with the attorney on Monday." He lifted the phone above his nose. *Dad*, he mouthed.

Ash gave a curt nod and scanned the room. In the center stood an enormous king-size bed now rumpled with a red and white bedspread and a matching blanket. A linen-covered headboard was attached to a rustic wood-slat accent wall. Crown molding shelves, stacked with garland and winter village, circled the room. The end table boasted a lamp and an artsy type Christmas tree. A dresser and a comfy chair in front of the fireplace finished off the room. A mirror image of his.

Eric hung up. "Are you out of your mind?"

A sigh rattled the back of Ash's throat. Ahh, guess the cat was outta the bag. That took longer than he expected. Maybe the whole inheritance business threw his dad off. "What'd I do now?" Pretty sure he knew the answer, but why make it easy?

"Weren't you at the Andrews County oil field recently?"

"I was." Yup. This was the one.

"You were supposed to fire Jackson for time lost, and instead, you lay him off and give him a year's severance package?"

Ash shrugged. No need to tell Eric that Jackson's kid had cancer and had been in and out of hospitals for months. Or that if Ash fired him, Jackson would lose insurance coverage. "The old man has been looking for a reason to get rid of me for years. If this is why he's going to fire me, I'm good with it. I'm going down for breakfast. I'm starving. You coming?"

Eric shook his head. "You got a backbone of steel, I'll give you that. I'll be down in a bit, I gotta call Lizzy and the kids. Save me some food."

"Tell them I said hi."

Ash knew to go against his father's wishes on the whole

Jackson fiasco was self-destructive, but he couldn't do it anymore. Couldn't blindly follow orders without thinking about the consequences. Jackson had been a good employee for years. It wasn't his fault his kid got sick. He needed the money and the insurance now more than ever.

Ash made it halfway down the stairs before his steps slowed. Something was off. Where were the anticipated aromas of bacon and fresh-baked bread? He didn't have much experience with the Bed and Breakfast scene, but breakfast would seem to be an essential part of the structure.

The dining room was empty except for an explosion of decorations. It looked like St. Nick himself unloaded his sack of Christmas all over the place. Every nook, cranny, and flat surface held a holiday decoration. But he did smell coffee. Finally.

"I can't believe you didn't tell us sooner." An angry female voice floated out from behind a closed door, followed by a bang.

"I didn't know until the day before yesterday."

"You could've told us at breakfast yesterday. Why didn't you?"

There was a mumbled reply and more cooking sounds. At least he hoped that's what they were doing. Ash turned to walk away when the next sentence stopped him.

"I didn't know how to tell you they were coming. Henri never mentioned any family." He recognized Quinn's voice. He moved closer to the door, coffee all but forgotten. Were they talking about him and Eric? Of course, they were. But why would they be this upset?

"I can't believe she would do this. What do you think it means?"

Whatever Henri did, it had these two women pretty worked up. He leaned in. For the longest time, Quinn didn't answer. He thought maybe he'd missed it, but there it was. Faint.

"I don't know what it means. For all I know it's out of our hands. Are you sure Henri never talked about a sister?" Quinn asked.

"I'm sorry. I don't remember her having any family."

A faint sizzle reached his ears, and a few seconds later, the wispy scent of bacon filled the air, and his stomach rolled right on cue. This wasn't right. He shouldn't be listening...

"What are they like?"

He moved further into the room.

"Well, I don't know... men."

The other woman laughed. "Are they young, old, cute, nice?"

More pans and background noises blocked the next comment to nothing more than a mumble. A couple more steps in, and he leaned forward to try and hear better. It sounded like... footsteps. Yup, someone was... *at the door*! He backed up and twirled to get out of the room before the door from the kitchen opened.

"Plan on something for dinner too. I'll figure out lunch."

If he could reach the hallway before—

"Ash?"

His foot tangled in a cord of Christmas lights and he took down the small lit tree that stood as sentry by the entrance to the dining room. *Who needed all these lights?* He righted the pot.

"How long have you been standing out here?" Quinn's tone sounded suspicious.

He made a slow turn and shrugged. "I came down for breakfast. And..." He glanced around, grasped for anything to explain why he stood there. "I smelled the coffee, and I tripped, and then, here you are. That coffee sure does smell good." He pointed to the coffee and made a beeline for the pot.

She stared with her mouth open. "Were you eavesdropping on our conversation?"

He deflated. "I didn't hear anything. I promise. I came in for breakfast, didn't smell anything cooking and heard the commotion."

She jutted her chin and scrutinized him. She must have decided to let it go because she didn't say another word on the subject. Instead, she waved him to the coffee.

"Breakfast will be ready soon. Carole Ann, she manages the kitchen at the diner, got here a bit late this morning." She poured herself a half cup of coffee, dumped in four heaping spoonfuls of sugar then filled it to the top with cream.

He hid a smile. The Angel... *oops, she doesn't like that name.* Quinn had a sweet tooth. Out of habit, he tucked that morsel of information away for future use.

"Have a seat," she said, her voice soft.

It tickled the short hairs at his neck. He pulled out the chair across from her and sat down.

"I take it Eric is not a morning person?" Quinn asked.

"Morning person, night owl, and a high-noon kinda guy." *A real energizer bunny.* "He'll be down shortly. Making the morning call to the family."

"That's right, he's married."

Was that disappointment in her voice? "Yes, with two terrific kids."

She sipped her coffee as the awkward silence grew.

"How about you? Do you have... I mean, are you married?" The sweetest blush crossed her cheeks.

"No. Happily a free man. Anyone special won your heart?"

"Not at the moment, no. Did you mean what you said last night?"

"You're going to have to be more specific, I said a lot of things last night."

"Are you and Eric going to sell to the ski resort?"

"If they want to buy, why wouldn't we?"

"Because," she blurted and then stopped for a breath. "Because, Henri, your aunt spent years pushing them away. All they want is the land. They'll come in here and tear this all down."

Pain flicked across her face and dulled the navy blue of her eyes to a stormy gray. Splotches of dusty pink bloomed on her cheeks.

Hmmm... dignified and pesky, had a spitfire core. Interesting. "What's wrong in that? Freshen things up, bring in new business, it will be a boon to this town."

"*This town* is doing fine. Thanks to the Wagners, who spent their lives building this from a fishing village to something that draws in the crowds. You should be proud of your heritage."

"First, I didn't know anything about this heritage until a week ago. Second, why do you care so much about it?"

Quinn stared into her coffee mug as if she searched for an answer to his question. Twin lines furrowed her brows.

"I'm sorry you knew nothing of Henri, she was a wonderful lady, and you would have loved her. Everyone does. Did. I care because..." She lowered her lashes and glanced away, but not before he caught the sheen of tears. "This town is a safe haven for a lot of people. In a world full of chaos and fear, we still keep our doors unlocked and our car keys stuck in the sun visor. The ski lodge wants to take that all away. Where would we go?"

"I'm sure the resort would hire them. And there must be other towns around here."

"You can't be serious." She tugged at her earlobe. "Did you not hear what I said? They want to tear it *down*. All of it.

Including the house. They don't care about the buildings or the people. They want the land. Your aunt worked to make this a family destination and draw the holiday crowds. The entire month of December is filled with holiday events that bring repeat business year after year. You don't throw that away."

Ash cringed. "An entire town built around Christmas. Don't you think that's overkill?" He flicked the holly leaves from the centerpiece. "Christmas is nothing more than an ad campaign to separate people from their money."

"My, aren't you a Grinch. You'd best be careful, or Santa won't be bringing you anything but a switch for your stocking." The twin spots of color returned to brightened Quinn's cheeks.

He hid a smile. He liked this side of her. A bit of passion flowed through those veins.

The door to the kitchen area banged open, and an older woman came through with a tray of food. The smell of pastries filled the air and made his stomach growl.

The woman placed the tray on the buffet, brought two of the three plates, and dropped one in front of him.

"Thank you. You're Carole Ann, correct?"

She stopped in her tracks. "Yes, and you are?"

Ash stood and held out his hand. "Ash Larsen. It's a pleasure to meet you." He turned up the southern charm and gave her his patented smile, guaranteed to make a woman swoon.

Her stance softened. "A pleasure. I guess. You're Henrietta's nephew?"

"Yes, ma'am, I am."

She dismissed him and took the second plate and dropped it in front of Quinn. She mumbled something like, you better fix this, before she walked back to the kitchen.

"She's a friendly sort." Ash picked up his fork, he didn't need an invitation. Hunger gnawed at his insides.

Quinn bristled. "Carole Ann is one of the sweetest people you'll ever meet. But she's not happy with me at the moment."

"Because you didn't tell her we were coming?" Too late, he realized his mistake.

"You *were* eavesdropping." Agitation creased her forehead. Plump, rosy lips puckered. "I knew it."

"Yes. Maybe, I overheard some of the conversation. It wasn't intentional, and, in my defense, neither of you were exactly talking in whispers. Plus, I was hungry. You may not be aware of this, but all red-blooded Texans eat meat. At every meal. And cheese, crackers and, grapes don't cut it."

A ghost of a smile tugged at her lips softening her face into something exquisite, her defenses gone.

"You have a beautiful smile." He regretted it immediately. Had no idea why he even voiced the thought, but the guarded expression she wore told him he'd stepped in it, right up to his ankles.

"Thank you." Her voice was faint, he had to strain to hear.

The next few minutes passed in silence as he devoured every crumb on his plate. He couldn't remember the last time he'd been that hungry. "Does Carole Ann do all the cooking for the B&B as well as the diner?"

"We have other cooks, but she plans the menus, the grocery lists, and does the scheduling for both places."

"You don't cook?"

She stood and picked up their dishes and walked to the door. "She is much better than I am. I'm guessing you and your brother are going to want a tour of the property?"

"That would be helpful, yes."

"I'll be ready at noon. My office is in the back. Meet me there." Then she disappeared through the door.

"I smell bacon. Please tell me I didn't miss breakfast." Eric hurried into the room a few minutes later.

"Nope, but you did miss the pre-meal show." Ash rose and got Eric's plate from the buffet. "Have a seat and let's talk."

Eric took three big bites before he came up for air. "Any coffee?"

"Behind you. Selling this place is not going to be that easy."

"Why?"

"Because there are going to be a lot of unhappy people around here if we do. That's why."

"Since when do we care about that? Besides, for every unhappy person, I can find at least one that will be thrilled." He inhaled the rest of his food and sat back. "I would think you of all people would be chomping at the bit to get the deal done. Getting this money keeps you from the marriage altar."

Ash's brow furrowed, but he said nothing. There wouldn't be a point. He couldn't argue with Eric when he was right about needing the money.

"Don't worry about it. Dad is sending another broker from Duluth. He'll be here Monday night after the first one leaves. The ski resort is still ready to buy. You're leaving here a much richer man than when you got here."

Ash wished he had his brother's confidence, but he couldn't shake the feeling the other boot still had to drop.

Chapter Five

Quinn paced her office in short, boxy steps trying to figure out her next moves. Niko chilled on his bed without a care in the world. "Lucky dog." At the sound of her voice, he thumped his tail against the wall in acknowledgment.

It was only the first morning, but after her conversation with Ash at breakfast, she got the impression they were dead set on selling.

"Knock, knock."

"Amy, what are you doing here?" Quinn stopped mid-pace and waved her friend into the office.

"Happy to see you, too. I talked to Carole Ann this morning. She said you were upset. I'm here to give you a pep talk." Amy dropped into the nearest chair and shoved her gloves in her pockets. "Are you wearing a hole in the carpet for a reason, or are you getting your step count up?"

Quinn stopped, and her lips twitched with a weak smile. "I wish it were one of the above." She collapsed into the chair behind the desk.

"Man trouble?" Amy wagged her eyebrows and leaned forward, chin propped in her hand.

"Yes. Two. Unwanted. And annoying."

"Well, I heard that at least one of them is all kinds of fine. And don't tell me you didn't notice. Carole Ann already told me you were glowing at breakfast."

"There was no glowing." Her nails cut into the palms of her hands. Ash may be tall and sinewy, with a gorgeous dream-worthy smile that should be outlawed, but the guy had a chip the size of Lake Superior strapped to his back

Amy quirked an eyebrow. "Liar much?"

Quinn jammed her fists under her arms to hide the white knuckles. "It... I... he was eavesdropping on our conversation. And if there was any glowing, it stemmed from anger. Nothing else."

"What were you talking about that he found so interesting?" Amy plucked her hair out of her coat collar. "Well?"

"I don't remember. Something about them and why Henri would've named them in the will. And how much. But honestly, why wouldn't she? They're family. But they don't have her memory or this town's best interest. What if she didn't... what if I don't have enough say to keep everything safe?"

Amy leaned back in her chair. "You were like a grand-daughter to her. There is a reason behind all this."

Quinn rubbed a throbbing temple and huffed out a breath. In her head, she knew Amy was right. Henri and Emerson never treated her like anything less than a grand-daughter. She never understood why they took her in when her family died. All anyone ever told her was they were friends of the family. She'd been thirteen. Alone and terrified when they rescued her from the fate of foster care.

"The way I see it, you have only one goal, convince these two they don't want to sell."

"And how do you expect me to do that?" Quinn tucked a stray hair behind her ear.

"That, my dear, is up to you to figure out." Amy stood and leaned over the desk to give Quinn a quick hug. "Don't look so glum. From what Carole Ann said, it could be fun."

"Would you stop?" A bruised and battered heart was a reminder of her history of bad choices when it came to men. She swore off the arrogant types a long time ago. Give her staid and steady any day. "I have no interest in him other than what he intends to do with this place." Monday couldn't get there soon enough. The *not knowing* was killing her.

Amy straightened and narrowed her gaze. "Henri must have had a good reason for what she did. You're going to have to figure it out and live with it."

Quinn snorted. "As pep talks go that one— not your best."

"Well, you didn't give me much to work with."

"Am I interrupting something?" Ash's already familiar voice tingled across her scalp.

He stood in the doorway, leaning against the frame arms crossed. A lazy grin of amusement crawled across his face, and male satisfaction oozed from every pore.

Her stomach muscles quivered in response.

Niko jumped up and trotted to him with his tail going in circles. Ash knelt and ruffled the dog's fur. Niko whined with pleasure.

Traitor.

How much of their conversation did he hear? She needed to be more careful. The man made a habit of popping up at the most inopportune times.

"Well, well, well, you must be one of those southern boys everyone's talking about." Amy stood toe to toe with Ash, giving him the once over. "I'm not sure yet what's going on here, but hear me well, this town needs Quinn and the Wagner's legacy. You best remember that." She slapped his chest with her gloves. "Don't make me remind you again."

"Yes, ma'am."

"Don't you have a diner to run, Amy?" Quinn asked.

"Yes, I do," she said as she sauntered out of the room. "I'll see you at dinner, Quinn."

"Seems like news travels fast around here." Ash gave his complete attention to Quinn.

You have no idea. "I guess you and Eric are ready for the tour?" She grabbed her winter gear off the hook.

"It's you and me for this round. Eric has some paperwork he needs to get done for my father before tomorrow morning."

"Oh, that's too bad." She slipped the coat back on the peg. "We can wait. I'm sure he'll want to see everything as well."

"He's gonna be a while and said to go on without him."

Quinn's mind struggled to find an excuse, any excuse, to keep from being alone with the man. Heat journeyed up her neck to end in, what she recognized from experience, would be a matching scarlet brand on her cheeks. She dropped her gaze and smoothed the sweater hem down her hips.

Too much like Ty. He'd made her uncomfortable in her own skin. Had been able to manipulate her. Ash threatened her way of life and everything she believed in. She couldn't afford to let him get in her head.

"Is that a problem?" His voice held genuine concern.

She was being silly. What did she think was going to happen? "No. No problem. Let me get my stuff again."

She slipped her arms into her coat and led him to the lobby. "You go get your gear, and I'll be in the kitchen when you're ready."

He glanced at his clothes and gave her a baffled expression. "I'm ready."

Quinn covered her mouth as laughter burst from her lips.

"You're joking." When she left her cottage earlier, it was negative fifteen with the wind chill.

He continued to stare at her, bemused. "What's wrong with this?" He plucked the collar of his jacket.

"You're wearing a windbreaker and," she lifted his hand, "where are your gloves?"

A smile spread across his lips with ease, pure male, and all confidence.

Playboy or not, the man could charm a tortoise out of its shell. Her heart jackhammered in her chest. *You're a shallow woman, Quinn McAllister.*

"I have these." He waved a pair of thin leather gloves under her nose. "And my boots." He lifted each foot for emphasis.

It was unthinkable that someone would actually come to northern Minnesota in December with nothing more than a windbreaker. She took solace in the fact the adventure wasn't going to last long.

He stepped aside and gestured for her to go ahead of him. "After you, darlin'."

For some reason, she couldn't explain, a mixture of anticipation and uneasiness made her movements stiff. They exited onto the tree-lined walkway at the back of the house before she led him toward her cottage and the path to the lake. Ice crunched beneath their boots, echoing in the chilled air.

"Your great-grandfather built this house in the nineteen twenties for his family. Henri used to say he was a modest man, calling himself a simple fisherman. The reality was, he came from money, and he took his inheritance and invested in his own fishing boats. Apparently, you come from a long line of people with good business sense because he sold out before the bust and moved his family back to the Twin Cities. They continued to use this as their vacation home." She stopped as the walkway met the lake path, right next to her cottage. "The B&B is named after him, Fisherman's Cottage."

She breathed in air so clean and crisp you could feel the cold to the very bottom of your lungs, and the exhaled moisture shimmered as glittery specks suspended in midair. In the spring, summer, and fall, her day started with coffee and a lakeside sunrise. Winter sunrises were breathtaking if you could stand the icy sting of wind as it blew across the lake.

The cold morning light bounced off ice shards and mounds, and bathed the harbor in silvery radiance. She could not have asked for a more majestic sight if she'd planned it.

Ash came to an abrupt halt. Would he be seduced by the beauty, or would he dismiss it as many people did? She chanced a quick glance from beneath her lashes. He stood with hands crammed in his pockets and hunkered into his coat collar. She couldn't be sure if he was impressed or turned off by all the frosty scenery.

"It's not often a Texan is left speechless, but here I am." His lopsided grin, as he turned to stare at her, warmed through her, and in that instant, her breath stilled as she recognized a kindred spirit.

"Makes me almost forget how cold it is," he said, spell broken. "*Almost.*"

She blinked repeatedly to clear her head and still her heart. "Wouldn't be so cold if you were dressed for winter rather than a walk on the beach."

"What are those? Out there on the ice."

"Icehouses. We don't normally have them out this early, but it's been a cold month."

"That's a real thing, huh?"

She giggled before she could stop herself. "Surely you've heard of ice fishing?"

"Of course. But I've never had an interest. I guess I didn't think about how it was done."

"See those two bright red houses to the left?" Her hand closed around his firm, muscled forearm. Shivers vibrated through the thin material. When he glanced at her hand, she dropped it as if she'd been singed and took a step back. "Those, um, they belong to us, well the B&B." She stumbled over her words and put more distance between them. "For guests who come here wanting a cold adventure."

"How many takers do you get?"

"You'd be surprised. Kids love it. There's always ice skating and snowmobiling to the local waterfalls."

"Now, that is something I'd like to do."

A flood of adrenaline rushed through her veins. Racing over the frozen ground around rough terrain to the waterfalls was one of her favorite pastimes. Being there, with the power of the water rushing over the side of the mountain. The frozen pool beneath. The giant ice-covered trees towering into the sky, it reminded her there was something more. Something bigger. The fact that this unwanted newcomer seemed to share her lust for adventure surprised her.

"Too bad you'll be leaving after your meeting on Monday." She directed him along the path next to the lake. "You know, there's more to us than winter. We have plenty of adventure for summer lovers, too."

"Oh, really? Name a few." He nudged her shoulder playfully.

"You can hike to the waterfalls, biking trails, gondola rides, swimming holes—"

"I get it. I do. The place has a lot to offer."

Ash gently squeezed her upper arm and steered her to the left of him, putting himself between her and the lake. They strolled along the path, both silent, lost in their own thoughts.

"Is that your cottage back there?" He nodded, keeping his hands shoved in his coat.

"Home sweet home."

He stopped. "It's beautiful. How long have you been here?"

"Mmmmm... most of my life. I lived down south, past Minneapolis, until I was thirteen. The only time I left was to go to school." She glanced around at the vast expanse of white, and her heart knew there would be nowhere else she could ever call home.

"Doesn't look like you get much nightlife up here."

"The ski lodge has a small casino and a couple of clubs. It's where the locals go. Most of our guests want something quieter, but some will head up there."

"And where do couples go for dates around here?"

"Grand Marais is not that far from here. Elf Hollow has a small movie tavern that serves dinner and shows second-run movies. There's also restaurants and shopping here and in nearby towns. We have everything that attracts people. The quiet and solitude with outdoor activities, close to skiing, hiking and bike trails, swimming holes in the summer." Excitement overcame her. The same way it always did when she talked about Elf Hollow.

"Where do your dates take you?" He kept his gaze straight ahead.

She stopped, her joy sinking into the snow. "Excuse me? I'm not sure what that has to do with anything."

He cocked his head and wagged his eyebrows. A conceited smile tugged at his lips. "Curious where our first date will be."

"What?" She spat out the single word. "What on earth gave you the impression we would be going on a date?"

He shifted on his feet. The smile he wore faded to confusion. "I... guess... I thought things were going well here. You can't deny we're having a moment. I assumed we would move to the next level."

She snorted her disapproval. "So, what? Every woman who shares a moment with you should hop into bed with you?"

"Whoa. I'm talking about a date. I never said anything about—"

"You didn't have too. I know your type, Ash Larsen. You're so superficial you think every woman is dying to drop at your feet."

"I assure you, I don't think anyone is dropping at my feet in this cold." He shrugged, and a smile meant to charm spread across his face.

Of course, he would find this funny. He was impossible. She pivoted on her heel and headed back to the house.

"Awwww, come on, Quinn. I was only joking. Don't leave."

She kept walking. Stupid. Stupid. Stupid. She'd learned her lesson the hard way. At least she thought she had. Handsome charmers were her kryptonite. They weaved their magic, and she fell under their spell. No way would she allow it to happen again.

"I'm sorry." Ash caught up with her and grabbed her arm to slow her down. His hand was firm, but he didn't hurt her. "I didn't mean anything. I'm sorry if I upset you."

Warm, golden gaze engulfed her, and she was horrified to realize she was mesmerized. "No." She shook his hand off. "You don't get to come in here, disrupt my life and everything I know and then charm your way through me." Been there done that. Had the broken heart as a reminder. She'd spent two years making excuses for Ty, even when all her friends tried to warn her. But he'd been sexy and sweet and funny. She didn't realize he was all those things for all women until it was too late. She was done with hot sexy men. Give her quiet, shy, and considerate any day.

He moved to stop her, and she put her hands up.

"Stop. Let me be. You're here for two more days before you plan on selling my home out from under me. Please, spare me the sorrys." She picked her way back to the house as quickly as she could over the icy path. The last thing she needed was him coming to her rescue.

She dodged into her cottage and watched out the window until he passed by. Her reaction had probably been excessive, but it really didn't matter. After Monday, he would be gone anyway.

Ash picked his way across the sidewalk turned slip-n-slide. What the heck happened? The woman was a baffling mix of cute, furry kitten and annoying tigress. One minute she was all sweet and cuddly. The next, she was ready to nip his hand off.

That was the problem with the cute, sexy, quiet ones... they could turn in a snap.

Chapter Six

Ash and Eric entered the attorney's office in Duluth, an hour and a half away, at nine-fifteen Monday morning. The old nondescript brick building, similar to all the others on the street, had nothing in common with the gleaming glass-encased offices of the attorneys their father employed in Houston.

The unimpressive exterior set the tone for the equally uninspired interior. No burnished marble, no glass walls. The only evidence of potential authority were heavy mahogany doors and cumbersome leather chairs that graced the waiting area. Neat and clean with a charm all its own, but nothing about the office screamed money or power. Prestigious wouldn't even describe the attorneys Henrietta Wagner chose to represent her in death. The flowery scent pumped from the mister on the counter couldn't mask the musky scent of old building.

Eric plucked a peppermint out of the bowl on the reception desk. "I really wish you would explain to me again how you managed to alienate Quinn. 'Cause I still can't figure it out."

He didn't answer. Eric had been hounding him ever since he came back to the house on Saturday.

"She was as friendly as a thorn bush when she came back from that walk. I all but had to beg her to stay and go over the books." Eric paused to tell the receptionist they were there. "What could you have possibly done to make her so angry?"

"Would ya let it go?" Ash had no answers. He'd asked himself the same question ever since she ran off and left him in the cold. *Literally.* His success with women was legendary. He could strut sitting down. And he knew women. How did he misread the signals? He would've sworn she wanted him. The sideways glance when she thought he wouldn't notice. The way she got all fired up whenever he came into the room. Even the fact that she ignored him in favor of Eric.

Maybe the cold interfered with his radar. Then again, Quinn surprised him. The women he dated wanted a good time. Status. Something he could give them. But Quinn wasn't like that. She saw right through him. He scrubbed a hand through his hair. He needed to get this inheritance mess done and go home. The deadline approached to put in his application for the restaurant location, and his ego had taken a hit. Nothing was right with the world up here.

"Mr. Fitz will see you now. If you'll follow me." The secretary led them down a dark hallway to the last door on the right.

An older man rose from behind his desk and extended his hand. "Gentleman, please come in, have a seat. I'm Harold Fitz, your great-aunt's attorney."

Ash didn't hear another word the man said. The caramel-haired woman who sat in one of three chairs lined in front of the desk commanded his attention.

"Quinn? What are you doing here?" He approached her, but she refused to give him the time of day. She had the air of a lost calf waiting for slaughter. Not at all like the spitfire from

45

the other day who told him off for no good reason before she left him to freeze like an ice sculpture at a wedding.

Eric stood next to him, bewildered. "Quinn?" He turned his attention to the attorney. "What's going on?"

"If you will both take your seats, I'm sure it will all begin to make sense."

Wide navy-blue gaze stared straight ahead, turning neither right or left. She pretended she was oblivious to the commotion. But he knew better. She knew exactly the shock her presence caused. Even white teeth sawed back and forth over her bottom lip. Legs crossed, hands clutched tight around the purse in her lap, knuckles white with strain. Dressed in black tights and white fuzzy boots with a flowered dress, she wore the disguise of delicacy, but he knew better than to fall for that.

"Why is she here?" Eric asked again.

"Mrs. Wagner requested she be here for this," the attorney said as if they should have known.

And the other boot drops.

Now, why would the manager need to be present for the reading of the will to the *beneficiaries*? Unless... A sense of disaster took root in his gut, turned the liquid to a rolling sea. What was it Granddad used to say? If it walked like a skunk and smelled like a skunk... Unease settled in the room.

"I'm confused. I was under the impression Henrietta had no children." Eric's tone was sharp. His jaw clenched until his teeth grated loud enough for all of them to hear.

"Are you ready to begin?" Mr. Fitz motioned Eric and Ash to chairs, then opened a cabinet and pulled out a TV. "Before we get started on the will, Mrs. Wagner recorded a message for all of you."

Ash moved his chair closer to Quinn before he took his seat. "Why didn't you tell us you would be here?" He whispered loudly in her ear. "You had plenty of opportunities."

"Mr. Larsen, please." The attorney leaned forward and put his elbows on the desk. "Ms. McAllister has no more knowledge than you. Mrs. Wagner made changes to her will very recently. Now, if you will allow me to begin?" When no one spoke, he pushed start.

A frail bird-like woman with white hair and pale blue eyes appeared on the screen. A stern, leaner version of Gran. Warmth flooded him. He stole a quick glance at his brother. A slight smile softened Eric's features.

"Hello? Do I start talking yet? What? Yes?'

Despite her frail appearance, her voice sounded strong and firm. Straightforward and matter of fact.

He leaned over and whispered to Quinn, "Is she your grandmother?" He neither expected or received an answer. He turned back to the screen.

"Well, if I'm up on that TV screen, that means Quinn, Ash, and Eric are in the same room together. And I'm dead. For Eric and Ash, I'm your great-aunt Henri. My sweet Quinn, I hope you are holding up. I know this must be very hard for you. Now to business."

"Why didn't you tell me you were related to Henrietta?" Ash whispered in Quinn's ear. It all made sense now. They were cousins. No wonder she stomped off horrified at his suggestion of a date. "All you had to do was tell me. I'm not some backwoods... I mean, I have no desire to date my cousin."

"Shhhh." She pinned him with a withering stare.

"Eric, Ash, you are the grandsons of my twin, Sadie. Despite running off with that boy, your grandfather, all those years ago and leaving me to face the humiliation, you're still family. I didn't think it was right not to pass on her inheritance. Never did buy into all that sins of the father mess."

Running off with that boy? Humiliation? She made it sound like some *Romeo and Juliet* scandal. That would imply a

47

deep, abiding love strong enough to endure the test of time. Something his grandparents, Sadie and Travis Larsen, never displayed. Ash always had the impression they barely tolerated each other. His grandfather was a hard man, much like Ash's father. He couldn't imagine anyone choosing to run away with that. What could have happened to change them?

"Sadie and I were born on December twenty-fourth. Every year, Fisherman's Cottage holds a combination Christmas/birthday party. It's quite an affair. We've had rooms booked since last December. Several of our guests will be returning as they have for many years." She smacked her lips. "Someone get me some water."

They all watched as a hand appeared on the screen and handed the old woman a glass. Ash stole a glance at Quinn. Were those tears on her cheek? His throat tightened. Whatever the relationship between the two women, it didn't take a genius to see they'd been close.

When his grandmother died, he'd lost the only person who ever loved him and accepted him. He wondered if Quinn had the same feelings for Henrietta. If she did, the loneliness of that loss would be unbearable. He had an irresistible urge to wrap her in his arms, absorb her pain. Offer comfort, but somehow he didn't think she would welcome the attention. Not from him.

"Thank you, that's better." Henri continued. "Here it is kids, a few rules to live by. There can be no sale, attempt to sell, or talk of sale to anyone until after January second. No exceptions. You got that, Mr. Fitz? As my attorney, you are in charge of making sure my wishes are met."

"She can't be serious." Ash launched from the chair, fists balled at his side. "Can she do this?"

"She can." Eric spat the words out between gritted teeth. "But why? Did she tell you why she was doing this?" Eric asked.

"I should think it's obvious. She's giving you boys the chance to do the right thing." Mr. Fitz paused the video with a heavy sigh.

Ash mentally listed his options. He'd planned to use his meager savings for the first and last month's rent when he signed the lease and use the sales contract to the ski resort as collateral for a start-up loan. There wouldn't be too many other chances like this. He kept digging himself deeper and deeper.

"Is there any way to fight the will?" Ash came back to his seat, calmer, but his skin itched and tingled as if it would burst at any moment.

"What's the matter with you two?" Quinn turned in her seat and speared them both with a menacing glare. "This is your legacy. Your family built that home. They're one of the founders of this town. Why am I the only one who sees this?" She slammed her purse on the corner of Mr. Fitz's desk as she rose and shoved the sleeves of her dress over her elbows before jamming fisted hands on her hips.

Did she intend to mimic a battle angel getting ready for a fight?

"Of all the self-centered, selfish, greedy—all you care about is the money. Never mind the lives involved. I can't for the life of me figure out why Henri trusted you two to care." A sob choked off the last word.

"Please," Mr. Fitz interrupted. "If everyone will calm down, we can let Henrietta explain."

When no one complained, he resumed the recording.

"For the next month, I want you boys to learn all about your family and what this place means to the valley. We're not just a bed and breakfast. Or a diner or a Christmas shop. We are a way of life for many people. We are the blood of this town. Eric, I understand from Sadie, you are the next in line to run your family's business. You have a lovely wife and two children. Far be it from me to keep you from all that." Her gaze drilled through him.

"Ash, on the other hand, prefers to live a more unconventional lifestyle with no rudder, no purpose."

His palms stung from digging his fingernails into them. Even a complete stranger saw through him and knew him as the joke of the family.

Henri's bird-like voice broke through his thoughts. "Since Ash doesn't have as much to lose, he will stay and learn everything there is to learn about all three of my enterprises. Furthermore, he will participate in all the planning and events."

Quinn gasped.

"If you do not follow this stipulation, Mr. Fitz here has the authority to complete the paperwork that will remove the two of you from the will." She stopped, sighed, and for a moment, her face radiated kindness. And regret. "I would've liked to have gotten to know you boys. Sadie thought the world of you both. Please don't prove her wrong."

The screen faded to black.

The three of them sat in stunned silence as they all processed what had happened.

What did she mean by *don't prove her wrong?* How would they do that?

Mr. Fitz cleared his throat. "To answer a few questions. Yes, she can do this. There are no gray areas or ways to get around it. Mr. Larsen, Ash, you will need to spend the month here. Eric, you are free to go. Then again, you both could choose to walk away from it all." He swirled in his chair and picked up a shoebox from the credenza behind him. The top bulged with its contents and had to be held together with a white ribbon. He handed it over to Quinn. "For your reading enjoyment."

"What's this?" She asked, face a stony mask of composure once again.

Mr. Fitz shook his head. "Not a clue, but Mrs. Wagner left no doubt about what to *do* with them. You were to get these today, and all of you are free to read them."

"Great. Now, where does Quinn fit in all this?" Ash glanced at her from the corner of his eye.

Mr. Fitz pulled off his glasses and tossed them on the desk. "Well, of course, Ms. McAllister inherits half of everything. She'll be there to show you everything you need to know and teach you about your family heritage. As your aunt instructed. And in the end, she's your... partner."

Ash opened his mouth to say something, but Eric slapped a restraining hand on his arm.

"My brother and I need a few minutes. Is there a room we could use?" All signs of irritation were gone and replaced by Eric's boardroom face.

Ash knew what that meant. His brother would be all business. The emotion, the personal side of things, wouldn't matter to him. He had a job he loved. Ash didn't even know if he still had a job.

"I'll have my secretary show you to the conference room."

Ash tilted his head to the side and contemplated the woman in front of him. She held his gaze. Sizing him up as he sized her up.

Neither Eric nor Ash said a word until they were alone and had closed the door behind them.

"We don't have much choice here, do we?" Ash started.

Eric rubbed a hand through his hair. "I don't know, maybe. From all the initial numbers it could be big." He paused, his gaze roaming to the window. "What are your thoughts? We could sign it all over to Quinn and be done. Even if we could sell it all today, it would be months before it goes through probate and the estate is settled. Besides, we came here under the mistaken assumption Henri had no other heirs. We're not going to take away as much as we first thought anyway."

Ash's chest hollowed. "All true. But this was my way out."

"You already have a way out. All you have to do is get married. All those women in your life. Pick one, and it's over."

Agitation dogged Ash's steps as he paced the room. He could've left Cayman Oil and his father's employ long ago. But he stayed out of family obligation. Hope that one day his father would accept him. Now, he was trapped in the fallout of his own recklessness.

"It's not a death sentence, Ash." Eric sighed.

"And what happens to the woman? I'd be tying her to a loveless marriage. I'd be no better than Granddad or Dad." Despite a lifetime of marriage, his grandparents had never been happy. And his father's third marriage to Maria was all show. He wanted more. Only he didn't know how.

"It's nice having someone to come home to."

"It's easy for you. You found someone you love and who loves you. Some of us..." He paused. "Some of us don't deserve that happiness."

"Fine. Whatever. You've got to convince Quinn it's in the best interest of everyone to sell. It's not going to be easy. She's made it very clear where she stands."

The doubt written all over his brother's face was a punch in the gut. Another person to let down.

"Can you do this?"

He thought of those navy-blue eyes, the smile he'd glimpsed at breakfast the first morning; when she spoke with passion about Fisherman's Cottage and all it meant to the town. *Could* he do this? He gave himself a mental shake. It's not like they were stealing anything from her, for god's sake. She owned half, in the end, she'd walk away with enough money she could start fresh anywhere in the world. Was that so bad?

Pour on the charm, show her the benefits of selling. He told himself it was for all of them. "Piece of cake."

They made it back to the room where Quinn now paced, the frustration evident in the stiff line of her body. The flared nostrils as she labored to breathe.

The tiniest seed of guilt took root, but he dug it out before he changed his mind.

"I'm in." Ash quirked an eyebrow at her and mustered all the swagger and confidence he could. "You ready for a challenge?"

Feet splayed. Hands fisted at her hips.

Wild. Beautiful in all her glorious fury. More importantly, a woman ready for the dare he just volleyed.

She tilted her head and notched her chin higher. "Bring it, *Cowboy.*"

Chapter Seven

Quinn leaned into her chair and rubbed the heel of her hands over dry, grainy eyes. Her lids scratched over her the corneas like salt in an open wound. The day had lasted five hours past its usefulness. After she left the attorney's office that morning, she'd come home to face the music. Not a pleasant experience. She'd rather gnaw through her right arm than go through that again.

To say the managers were stunned would be an understatement. Everyone reeled from the knowledge Henrietta had a family. And she left them half of everything. On top of all that, Quinn had to explain they needed to work with and be friendly to Ash. Help him to see the beauty of Elf Hollow for the charming place it was.

But their annoyance at her for not sharing when she first got the letter from the attorney was the worst part. She'd hurt them.

An icy-blue ball of hopelessness flared in the pit of her stomach, and her mouth went dry. A sensation that repeated itself every few hours if she focused too long on the events of the day.

The boys would sell their half to the ski lodge the minute the month ended. Then she'd be the only defense this town had against the glitzy modernization the lodge wanted. Life would become one constant battle, and how long before the resort's deep pockets ran her finances out?

Quinn's only hope was to convince Ash and Eric the better gamble would be to keep the properties. At least until she figured out how to raise the money to buy their share.

She huffed out a deep breath and glanced at the chaotic mess on the desk. Henri held a strong distaste for computers and insisted everything be done with paper and pen—which created more work to put together the events for the month. There was still so much to complete before their first guests arrived next week. Unless she counted Ash as a guest, and she didn't. She counted him as a thorn in her side. A thorn she was not at liberty to remove thanks to Henri's bizarre mandate.

She was so angry at Henri. Why would she do this? Quinn understood the whole family obligation thing, but Sadie walked away from all this years ago.

Her stomach growled with the reminder she'd missed dinner. She checked her phone. Ten o'clock. She tilted her head against the back of the seat, limbs heavy in defeat. Carole Ann left a plate of the night's special in the fridge before she'd headed home. The idea of warmed-over meatloaf was about as appealing as tree bark, and she was too tired to walk home and nuke something.

Quinn's gaze flickered to the shoebox on the corner of her desk. The white ribbon barely kept the papers contained. She leaned forward, cleared a space, and pulled the box closer, nibbling at her lip. Did she want to know what was inside, or would it be better to keep her head buried in the sand?

The most delicious scent floated through the office door. Her mouth watered like Pavlov's dogs, and her stomach rumbled.

Seconds later, Ash walked in with a tray filled with food, a single rose, and two candles.

What brand of torture was this? Her chest tightened, and her breath shallowed.

"Late night snack time." A mischievous smile brightened his face.

Nerves tingled like a thousand butterflies hovered above her skin. She licked her lips and eased back in her chair. Tall, tanned, honey of a man with strong, broad shoulders, carried a tray filled with seduction. She wasn't strong enough to cope with that.

"I noticed there wasn't much food in the fridge. I made a supply run on my way back from taking Eric to the airport." He stopped at the corner of the desk and waited.

"What?" Her voice cracked. A warm, hazy fog washed out rational thought in a brain gone suddenly numb.

"Are you going to move those papers, or should I assume they are disposable and put the tray on them?"

She scooped all the papers together and shoved them off to the side. "Um... Right."

"For a bed and breakfast, I'm surprised at the lack of food supplies."

She blinked a few times and rolled the chair back as he placed the tray down next to her. "Blow the candles out, please."

"Why?"

"Because I asked you to that's why." Her voice trembled, and she had to clear her throat to try again. "I don't like the smell. Please, blow them out." She turned her gaze from the flames and prepared herself for the nausea that always followed the scent of an extinguished candle.

He cocked an eyebrow in question, but he did as she asked and moved them to a shelf without a word.

The tension between her shoulder blades eased, and she moved close enough to see the food on the tray. "You cook?"

"Are you hungry?" He ignored her and unloaded the tray.

"No. I ate something earlier."

"Liar."

The urge to slap the smug off his face shocked her normally passive nature.

"Carole Ann told me before she left, there was food in the fridge for both of us."

Drat. Of course, she did.

"And since I've been in the kitchen since she left, and I haven't seen you..." he tsked around an unrestrained smirk. The man was too cocky even when he didn't try. *Infuriating.*

"Fine. I'm not hungry." Her traitorous stomach chose that moment to contradict her words.

"Really? You hate me that much that you'd rather starve than eat the food I made?" He waved the plate under her nose. Taunted her with the heavenly aroma.

She salivated and swallowed. "I don't hate you." She took the food. "I find you highly annoying."

He poured them each a glass of wine and took the seat across the desk from her.

With reluctance, she took a bite of the sandwich. An explosion of flavors hit her taste buds all at once. Sweet. Savory. Warm, creamy cheese. "Oh my goodness, what is this?"

"Bacon, Brie, and apricot grilled cheese with balsamic reduction." A gratified grin slid across his lips.

The mean girl in her searched for something to criticize, but another bite of the ambrosia he called grilled cheese shut her right up.

"How does a bed and breakfast operate with no food in the kitchen?" He shook out his napkin on his lap.

She swallowed and took a sip of wine before she answered. "Not that hard, really. We've had no guests since Thanksgiving. I grab something when I think of it. When we have guests, Carole Ann or one of the cooks brings the breakfast up here from the diner, or they bring the food up to cook. But we only serve breakfast and snacks. It's not that hard to pull off." She polished off the first half of the sandwich and wiped her hands on the cloth napkin he threw at her. "The better question is, where did you learn to cook like this?"

"Ahh. *That* was a dare laid down in my senior year of high school. A friend and I both have, shall we say, *difficult* relationships with our fathers. What better way to tick off power-driven, money-hungry men than for their sons to tell them they are going to culinary school?"

"You went to culinary school?" A giggle bubbled up as her thoughts flashed on an image of him in a huge, fluffy white chef's hat and red and white checkered apron.

"Hey! Why is that so hard to believe?"

"I had a flash of you decked out in all your chef finery."

"And that made you laugh?" Humor released the tension in his expression, and seriously, how on earth was a woman expected to ignore the deep, sexy dimple in the side of his mouth?

She shoved a corner of the sandwich past her lips before she could say something she would regret. He was already a vexing combination of confidence and conceit. She didn't need to give him anymore encouragement.

He lifted the silver lid off the last dish. "Dessert."

Pound cake, raspberries, and chocolate sauce. Pure torture. She couldn't remember the last time she ate like this.

Handing her a spoon, he motioned for her to take the first bite. "And yes, I went to culinary school for a year and then moved on to Texas A&M. But not before I discovered a love of cooking. It served me well, and I found that co-eds loved a man who cooked."

She took a spoonful of the silky dessert. Rich, decadent,

chocolate slipped over her tongue, and this time she allowed the groan of pleasure. If he gave this dreamy confection to those co-eds, it was no wonder they loved him.

"What was Henrietta like?" He cocked his head to the side and rubbed a hand over his chest. "Gran was gentle, you know? She was always there in the background making sure everyone had what they needed." His gaze dimmed as if lost in the past.

Not wanting to interfere with his thoughts, she opened and closed her mouth. Did she say something or leave him to his memories? "Ah... Feisty would be the best word to describe Henri. You saw the video this morning. Don't get me wrong, everyone loved her, and she loved everyone around her, but she reserved the softest part of herself for those closest to her."

His gaze roamed over her with an intensity that overwhelmed her. "What about you? Who was Henri to you? Did you see her softer side?"

An innocent question, but one that brought up so many memories. And questions. A month ago, Quinn would have sworn she knew everything there was to know about her benefactress. Now?

She shook her head. Chanel No 5, frugal Henrietta's favorite perfume, settled in the room. The raspy warmth of the old woman's hand brushed Quinn's cheek as she had so many childhood nights. "She and Emerson were surrogate grandparents. They never had children of their own. When my parents died, they took me in. I thought I knew her. But honestly, how well do we know anyone? I mean, look at you. You must have been close to your grandmother, right? And yet here you are in the dark as much as I am."

He tilted his head, "Yeah. As close as anyone, I guess. I spent more nights with her and Granddad than I did at my house. As a single parent, my dad could only handle one kid at a time, and Eric won that battle."

"Why not stay with your mother?"

Sadness cloaked him like a gray cloud and blurred the usual charming mask he kept firmly in place. "My mother died a long time ago."

She swallowed past the lump in her throat, the loss of her own mother as fresh as if it happened yesterday. Searching for something to ease his sadness, she latched onto the only thing she could think of. "What did she look like? Your grandmother?"

He rewarded her efforts with a real, genuine smile. Not one of those fake ones he always hid behind.

Heat spread through her veins from her head to her toes. Tremors rode along her spine, making her skintight and itchy... she choked on the next thought and shut it down. No need to unpack *that* bag. He was a playboy, nothing more. Best she remembered that.

"Identical, yes," he replied.

"It makes you wonder what happened between them. I mean, your grandparents up and left without another word to anyone. They left everything. It had to be something dreadful." Quinn rubbed her ear. Emerson had to know, but if he did, he'd kept his wife's secret.

"I haven't a clue. The way Henri referred to my grandparents made it sound like they had some great romance thing. But, I'm not even sure they liked each other. Eric and I thought they were both born and bred in Texas. She was the picture of a southern belle."

Quinn pulled the shoebox front and center. "Maybe we'll find answers in here."

Ash stared at the box. "Yeah. But do we want to know what those answers are?"

She opened the box. "Letters. It's full of letters."

They pulled a few out and read through them. All of them were from Sadie.

"It's strange," Ash said.

"Yeah, all these years they'd been writing, but they never told anyone about the other. I wonder why?" She dropped a stack of letters back in the box.

"Hopefully, something in there will answer the mystery."

They spent the next couple of hours deep in conversation and laughter. Compared notes about the sisters. Speculated on the reason for their split.

The clock in the hall chimed midnight. They'd lost all track of time.

"Wow, I didn't realize how late it was. I should probably get back to my place." Quinn stood and loaded the empty dishes on the tray. A swarm of emotions swirled through her head. Reluctance to end their conversation slowed her movements, and caution rang like a warning bell in her head. She needed to guard her thoughts before they could become words between them.

"I'll take those." He offered.

"That's okay, it'll only take a minute to load the dishwasher."

His warm hand circled her arm. "Quinn, I got it. I'm supposed to help around here. Remember?"

She hesitated, but then remembered he wasn't a guest anymore. "Okay, but don't leave it. I already told Carole Ann we didn't need her in the morning."

"Don't you eat breakfast?"

"I usually nuke something with my coffee. If I'm hungry, I go to the diner."

"Come on. I'll walk you back to your place."

"You don't have—"

"I know I don't have too." He handed over her coat. "I want to. My coat's in the kitchen I'll grab it on the way out."

The incessant wind dragged the very air from her lungs the second she stepped out the back door. She cast a quick glance at Ash in his wanna-be winter jacket and no gloves or hat. "Really. It's too cold out here for you. I'll be fine."

"Haven't you heard? Us Texans can handle anything," he said around the quiet chatter of his teeth.

They walked to her cottage, and she turned to smile at him. "Thanks for dinner. It was probably the best meal I've had in... forever. But you can't tell anyone, especially Carole Ann."

"It was my pleasure, and I promise it'll be our secret. I'll meet you for coffee in the dining room at eight?"

"Yup. It's a date." She took a step, stopped and spun on her heel "Wait, that's—"

"No take backs, Quinn."

Ash hurried back to the house, cursing the nasty temperature every step of the way. He couldn't wait to get back to Houston. No idea how these people lived with this god-awful weather. But on the lighter side, dinner had been enjoyable. With all the tension that could have bounced between them, neither of them used it. Maybe they'd been feeling each other out. An unspoken truce. Whatever it was, he liked spending time with her. For no other reason than she was... *fun*.

Quinn was cute with her wide, innocent smile, and her wholesome, too-good-for-him kinda charm. Her beautiful, trusting blue eyes cast a web of magic over him. It was the only explanation for why he'd enjoyed their evening as much as he had. Quinn was the embodiment of the women he avoided at all costs. Her kind expected too much.

He shivered and pushed all the cuteness out of his head. No adorableness. He'd be gone in a month.

Cold seeped into his bones. The weight of fatigue made his feet heavy, like slogging knee-deep through a muddy river.

First the meeting, and then the drive to and from the airport, followed by a late-night meal.

He entered the kitchen and hung up his coat before rolling up his sleeves. Grabbing the washcloth from the edge of the sink, he read the statement *Happy Merry Christmas* with a wreath tucked on either side. *Good Lord, seriously?* There was a fine line between holiday enjoyment and holiday fanatic. These people had blown way past that line.

He surveyed the mess he'd created and threw the washcloth back in the sink. He'd been up since seven, drove eight hours back and forth to the airport, and prepared dinner. This mess wasn't going anywhere. It was time for bed, he'd take care of it first thing in the morning.

Chapter Eight

T he next morning, Ash strolled into the dining room. Muttered curses floated from the kitchen, followed by the sound of plates being dropped into the sink. He cracked the door to peek around the corner.

Quinn glared at the mess from the night before. Hands gripped her hips as if that was the only thing that kept her from knocking the tray he'd left in the office overnight onto the floor in disgust.

Well, dang. "Good morning," he said as he came through the door. Maybe if he forced cheerfulness, she would take his cue.

She offered him a scowl that burned brighter than a road flare and threw the pan she'd picked up into the sink.

"About this." He waved his hands. "I can explain."

"And what can you explain?" She asked in a calm, rational tone. "The reason you left this mess for someone else to clean, even after I specifically told you we had no one coming in to do it? Or perhaps you want to explain why someone else should clean it up?"

She was taking this all wrong.

"I didn't expect you to get it."

"Who did you think would do it? I told you no one was coming this morning." Her voice no longer sounded rational, but she stopped for air and ground her teeth. "Ash, we have a lot of work to get done before our guests arrive at the end of the week. You asked me to trust you to handle it. But you left it for someone else."

"I'm sorry. I planned on getting them first thing this morning. It was a long day. I was tired."

"I have a list longer than both arms I have to complete before I can lay my head on the pillow tonight. And you've added," she scanned the room, "at least forty minutes to my day." She moved toward the stove.

He stopped her with a soft grip to her shoulders. "Stop. Please. I'm sorry. I didn't realize first thing in the morning started with sunrise. You don't need to bother with this. I got it. The last thing I want to do is add to your workload."

She pressed her lips in a tight line. "Fine." She reached around and untied the apron she wore over a pink fuzzy sweater and dropped it over his head. "Feel free to get it done now. When you're finished, you can head over to the Christmas Shoppe. The manager there, Jim Lovett, is waiting for you. And for the record, around here, the day starts *before* sunup." She stormed past him and shoved through the door, the scent of fresh rain in her wake.

Truce didn't last long. He held up the apron. Red with a torso-sized Christmas tree. *Of course.* He shrugged and tied it around his waist before he opened the dishwasher and got to work.

Two hours later, Ash hauled another load of Christmas ornaments from the backroom of the Christmas Shoppe and dropped them onto the table. After he'd finished at the house, he checked in with Jim Lovett. A man who held nothing but contempt for Ash.

He stretched his back and surveyed the store, surprised to see all the activity. In this day and age he'd been under the belief most people shopped online. But customers had packed into the place since he arrived. Guess there were still people out there who enjoyed this stuff. A good sign for whoever bought the place. So far, it was the only business that brought in a steady stream of cash, but in all fairness, he hadn't been to the diner yet. The B&B was more seasonal.

"Larsen," Jim barked as he swept by. "When you're done with those, get them all on the shelves and then bring out a few more of those artificial trees."

Ash glared at the manager's retreating back. The tedious responsibilities Jim assigned him were mind-numbing and not what he had in mind when Henri told him to stay and learn.

Ash lost count of how many times the man had told him he didn't belong there. It wasn't hard to see where the man's loyalties rested.

"Ash, don't stand there. Take one of those boxes to the register. There's a customer waiting." Jim bustled by on his way to the back. The man was rugged, with a clean-shaven head, neat, gray beard, and well-muscled frame. Ash figured he was somewhere in his fifties, and judging by the reaction of the women who came in the store, he was attractive. And he was a pain in Ash's neck.

Ash walked the box to the young girl at the register. She gave him a shy smile, and a breathy *thank you*.

At least someone here liked him.

"Aren't you old to be a stock boy?"

The throaty voice rescued him from the negative vibes in his head. He glanced over his shoulder to see a sultry redhead decked out in full snow bunny gear. She twirled a strand of hair, a coy smile on her lips.

He fell right into his role and gave her a cocky grin. "Stock boy? Angel, I'm the owner." *This* was familiar territory. *This* he knew how to handle. "Can I help you find something?"

"I want a new pair of boots. White with white fur. Do you have anything like that?"

He rested his hand at her lower back and guided her to the shoe section. "I'm sure we can find something that meets your needs. Do you live here in town?"

"No, I'm here on a ski trip. I'm staying at the ski lodge. Do you ski?"

He pulled two pairs off the shelf. *Never.* "Yeah, I've been known to go down a few slopes."

"Maybe I'll see you up there sometime. I'm here for the rest of the week."

It was doubtful he would get much time for the slopes. "How do these look?"

She contemplated the pairs he held for her perusal. A red-tipped finger pointed to the one on his left. "These."

She was an open book, telecasting her wants and needs for anyone to pick up on if only they paid attention. But he needed to keep his focus. He had a goal beyond his own needs. A sale. Once again, in the role of trying to prove his worth. Something he'd spent his entire life doing. This time to the store manager.

He got her size and headed to the stock room. A few minutes later, the woman preened in front of the full-length mirror.

"Those boots are perfect on you." He let the words tangle with a gruff drawl. A sound guaranteed to shiver over a woman.

She peeked at him from beneath her lashes and ran a finger down her throat, then turned back to admire the boots against her pink ski pants. "They're perfect. I'll take them." One more glance before she turned her attention back to him. "I'll wear them out. Pack those old ones up in the box."

He walked her to the register, pleased he'd managed to contribute something beyond stocking shelves. A small victory, but he'd take it.

A loud noise, like a table shoved across the floor, echoed from the other side of the store. It was followed by the tinkle of glass shards as they danced and pinged on the hardwood.

"Ashlyn Marie, I told you to keep your hands to yourself." A woman's harried voice floated throughout the store. That didn't sound good. No doubt the boxes of ornaments he'd been carrying out of the stock room, now lie in a crushed pile at little Ashlyn Marie's feet.

A red-faced Jim charged over to him. "Ash, did you stock the ornaments onto the shelves like I asked?"

"Ah, I was helping this customer find a pair of boots." He handed the box over to the girl at the register and gave the woman a tight-lipped smile, holding on to a semblance of dignity. But his insides churned with indignation.

"See you around, handsome." She smiled and wagged her fingers.

Ash nodded and waited for her to leave before he faced Jim. "I'm not any happier about this setup than you are. I have a life back in Houston. I'm here on the whim of a woman I didn't know existed until a month ago. We've been thrown together, but let's be clear. I'm not one of your clerks." Ash took a deep breath, tried to remember his aunt put him here, not Jim. Neither of them were thrilled by the situation.

The two stood toe to toe in a staring contest before Jim assessed him. His face softened. "Let's go to my office."

After the door closed, Jim motioned Ash to a chair. "You and your brother are planning to sell your share, right?"

The question threw him off, and Ash scrambled for a response. "I thought we were going to duke it out."

"I think we covered that out on the floor. In front of everyone. You're right. I didn't give you a fair shot. Didn't want you here. Still don't. Most of the people you'll meet, including me, believe Quinn should inherit this business. *All* of it. But Henri was loyal to a fault. Even to relatives she never acknowledged in life." He sat back in his chair. The silence grew between them.

Ash squirmed in his chair. "I had nothing to do with any of that. I'm sure you've already heard about the mystery."

"I can't read you. And I'm a good judge of character. But I'm willing to start fresh. I've worked for Emerson and Henrietta for many years. I've known Quinn since she showed up here fifteen years ago. Broken and alone. I count her as family. I'm sure Henri had her reasons for all this. I suspect she hoped you'd find something here. Something that would keep you from selling off her life's work."

Ash zoned out, brought short at the broken remark. Quinn couldn't have been more than twelve, thirteen maybe? "How did Quinn end up here?"

"Have you listened to anything I said?" Annoyance oozed from Jim.

"Yes. I'm supposed to learn and gain some mysterious thing from being here. Got it." He crossed his arms and waited for the other man to decide if he'd answer him.

Jim rubbed his finger across his upper lip. He seemed to reach a conclusion when he sat forward and steepled his hands, elbows on the table. "Quinn lost her family at thirteen. The Wagners were family friends. They never had children of their own and didn't have the heart to see her go to a foster home. Satisfied?"

Ash gave him an absent-minded nod, his forehead wrinkled. Quinn lost her family when she was a child. Emerson and Henri were the only family she'd had. Now they were both gone. How was she holding up with everything on her plate? She hadn't even had time to grieve, yet they all expected her to have it together.

"Okay, let's start fresh. I don't want you here, Henri did. So, we have to figure out a way to work together." Jim stood, ending the strange conversation. "I'm headed to lunch. The shop's yours. Don't screw it up."

He walked out, leaving Ash to wonder what he'd talked himself into.

An hour later, he'd cleaned up the mess from the dropped ornaments, reorganized the end caps to freshen things up and straightened the shoe section. Not one customer showed up in that time. What happened to the crowd?

He pulled out his black notebook. Most people assumed the black book held his list of women, and it served his purpose to let them continue to think that.

He opened the personal recipe book to the last page, *veal and mashed potatoes.* When the day came, he'd have a long list of recipes to build a strong menu. But for now, he needed one perfect meal.

Cooking was his superpower, and in the past, he hadn't always used that power for good. Tonight, he could do something to make someone else happy. For no other reason than the sheer joy of a smile. The kind Quinn used to chase the winter chill from a room.

The phone rang and pulled him from his thoughts. "Ash, let me talk to Betsy."

"She is not here yet, Jim. What's up?"

"Right. She's not due into for another forty-minutes. My grandson is sick, and I have to go pick him up. I won't be coming back. Have her call me when she gets in. I need to go over a few things."

"I'm here now. How about you tell me what you need?"

"I think it's better I talk with Betsy."

Ash puffed out a sigh of frustration. "Cut me a break. We just talked about this. I'm capable of taking care of the store and all its responsibilities."

A long pause greeted him from the other end. "You're right. I'm sorry. We need to get the Christmas tree order in by tonight for them to deliver our first order of trees by Saturday morning."

Ash pinched the bridge of his nose. Did *everything* in this darn town come down to Christmas? "Will Santa and the reindeer be here, too?" He didn't bother to hide the sarcasm. *For the love of Christmas* took on a whole new meaning.

"Yes, along with an elf."

The man wasn't joking. "Well, then. Wouldn't want to disappoint Santa, now, would we? What do you need me to do?"

"On my desk is the web address and all the information for the tree farm. I've already completed our numbers. All I need you to do is place the order by eight o'clock tonight. We've bought from this farm for years. No need to worry about payment. They'll bill us."

The door opened, and the redhead from earlier in the day sauntered in. Her hips swayed in slow, seductive circles as she approached him. The woman sure used the gifts God gave her.

"Hello, handsome," she purred.

"Ash? Did you get all that?"

"Yup. Got it. Place the order by eight, they'll bill us. Hope your grandson feels better."

"Thanks. And thanks for taking care of this."

Ash hung up and gave his full attention to the woman in front of him. "The boots look good."

"They feel good. Everyone loves them. I thought I would come here and thank you personally. What are you doing later? I'm staying at the resort. Some friends and I are throwing a party."

His first thought was *yes, finally,* something to do in this town, then he glanced at the notebook in his hand. A laughing Quinn from the night before floated somewhere in his thoughts. Always doing the right thing in spite of the obstacles. The grief. "You know, a week ago, I'd have been all over the invitation. And I appreciate it. But I think I'm going to pass." A tranquil warmth flooded through him. This is what it felt like to rise above his own wants.

Forty-five minutes later, as Ash swept the floor in front of the entrance, a snowmobile came down the side of the road and plowed to a stop. A spray of snow dotted the sidewalk. Finally, something more interesting than a dust particle to be swept.

Ash opened the door as Betsy removed her helmet and climbed off the back of the snowmobile. "Johnny, I told you not to do that."

"I'll clean it up, mom. Don't worry."

"That was cool," Ash said.

"Hello, Ash. This is my son, John. John, this is Ash Larsen, one of Henri's nephews."

The man took off his helmet, grinned, and held out his hand. Dark hair, tanned, from hours outside, he appeared to be about Ash's age. And the first person he'd met to give him a genuine, nothing-to-resent greeting. "Yea, we haven't met, but I work for Fisherman's Cottage. Tech work for the B&B, general cleanup, maintenance kind of work."

Ash walked around the vehicle. "You ride this thing through town?"

"The plows leave a ride strip down the sides of the roads for us. Some of us prefer to get around like this."

"Love it."

"Ever ride?"

"Not much call for these in southeast Texas."

"I'm headed up to the resort. I have a rider up there. Side gig. I'd be happy to take you up."

"Serious? Heck, yea."

"Mom, can he borrow your helmet?"

"Of course."

"Let me grab my coat." Ash headed back into the store. Excited to experience snowmobiling for himself. And, it didn't hurt he'd have a chance to check out the competition.

He grabbed his coat and headed to the front where Betsy was set up behind the register. "You going to be okay here by yourself?"

"I do it every day, son. I'll have help coming in the next little while. Go on and have a good time. Johnny is the best trail guide there is. You'll have to go with him one day for that."

"Thanks, Betsy."

By the time he was back out front, John already had the sidewalk cleared off and waited for him.

"It's gonna get cold. But you're going to love it."

"What are we waiting for? Let's get this party started."

Chapter Nine

Quinn came through the door of the Christmas Shoppe Saturday morning after she received an urgent call from Jim. He needed her ASAP, that's all he would say. An unusual request from her calm, unflappable manager.

"Quinn, back here," Jim called and motioned her to the back windows, concern marring his face.

She searched for Ash as she maneuvered through the throng of early shoppers. She knew from her conversations with Jim, Ash didn't like all the Christmas joy, and would be happier working anywhere else.

A tinge of guilt niggled at her for dumping him there all week. At the time, it seemed like the right thing to do. Out of sight, out of mind. She didn't even know where to begin with him. How do you show someone the beauty of something, when they hate the entire principle of the very thing? Ash Larsen hated Christmas. Someone like that wasn't going to change. Unless she could find out *why* he hated it so much.

"We have a problem." Jim interrupted her thoughts, a scowl on his face.

"Okay. I'm sure whatever it is, we can figure it out."

"We have no trees." Simple and to the point.

Her gaze traveled to the scene outside where Santa's tent stood and lines formed. The ice-covered lake sparkled beyond. The split-rail fence next to the tent, eerily empty. "Where are they?"

Jim shrugged. "You tell me. I left instructions for Ash to place the order on Tuesday."

"Okay. Not a problem. Let's talk to Ash."

"That would be nice. But he's not here. I'm sorry, Quinn. I should have followed up. I knew he wasn't capable of handling this. It's my fault."

"Stop. You should be able to trust a grown man to get the job done."

She frowned and tried to keep the alarm bells to a quiet roar. Tree day brought in a big chunk of their revenue for the season. It helped fund the donations and the North Shore Retirement Home's party.

"Are you sure? Maybe he placed the order—."

"Quinn, do you see trees out there? I don't see trees. We open in an hour, and there's not one tree on the lot. We have a Santa, we have an elf, we even have a reindeer, and thanks to Amy and Carole Ann, we have hot cider and cookies. What we don't have are trees."

Quinn glanced out the back window for the tenth time. *Think. Think. What would Henri do?* Henri wouldn't have allowed this to happen.

The fault fell on her. She'd avoided Ash all week. Instead of working with him as Henri wanted, she'd pawned him off on Jim. All because she got her nose bent out of shape over dirty dishes. At least that was the excuse she told herself. It was easier than admitting the dinner had been enjoyable way beyond the food.

"You know I wandered into town about a month after this

place opened." Jim crossed his arms and fell against the wall. "I was young, no ambition. But Emerson saw something in me. Gave me a job and a place to stay. He convinced me to stay awhile."

"I remember the story. Emerson used to talk about what a find you turned out to be."

"Did he also tell you he introduced me to my wife?"

She shook her head. Somehow, she didn't think Jim needed an answer from her.

"Ally worked in the diner waiting tables. Emerson used to send me over there with every excuse under the sun, but only when Ally worked. He needed coffee, or lunch, a sudden need for something sweet." He chuckled at the memory. "She was beautiful with her fiery red hair and freckles over every inch of her face, I'd get all tongue-tied whenever she was around."

"She's still covered in freckles," Quinn said.

"I was terrified to ask her out. Late one night, during inventory, Emerson asked me to go to the diner and get him a piece of pie. When I got there, Ally waited with a candlelight, dinner." He spared her a glance, nostalgia etched across his face. "My entire life, everything good, came out of this place. I don't have a clue where I would go from here."

Quinn didn't know what to say. Ash's presence had many people on edge and in need of answers. Answers she didn't have.

"Hey, what are you doing here?" Ash asked as he came up behind them. "You've been avoiding me."

"Where have you been? I've been trying to call you for the last hour." Jim launched from the wall, his face red with anger.

Quinn gripped his arm with a reassuring squeeze. "It's okay. Why don't you see if we can get Santa started? Keep the crowd occupied."

He gave Ash one last scowl before he stalked off.

"What's got him all worked up?"

"Ash, come with me to the office," Quinn snapped.

"Why have you been avoiding me?"

Because it's easier to avoid than face the problem. Everyone knows that. Quinn ignored him until they got to the office.

She waved him into the chair. "What day is today?"

His forehead wrinkled, and his lips pulled into an uncertain smile. "Saturday."

She raised an eyebrow. "Anything else?"

"I'll bite. What is today?" He swiped a hand across the base of his neck.

"It's tree day."

He gave her a blank stare. "Okay."

"It's hard to have tree sales with no merchandise."

"That's crazy I ordered them on Tuesday —" Red crept up his neck, and he reeled back. "I didn't order the trees. Quinn, I'm sorry. I... I don't know what to say."

"What happened, Ash? Jim said he left you the information. All you had to do is upload the final numbers."

He shoved himself from the chair and paced the small office, something she knew he did when agitated.

"I got sidetracked."

"I realize this place, this town, means nothing to you, and you've made it painfully clear you think all this Christmas buzz borders on a joke. But it means everything to a lot of people around here. You thumbed your nose at all of us." She pinned him with a glare.

"What's the big deal? We'll make a call and have them here by tomorrow. It's trees."

"*Christmas* trees. Tomorrow won't work. What about all the people, all the *kids* that made the trip today to find the perfect tree? Let's send them to the next town to buy their tree."

He dropped into the chair, and for the first time, a real expression of understanding dawned on his face. "I'm sorry.

For what it's worth, it wasn't intentional. What can I do to fix this?"

"You've done enough. I'll make a phone call and see if I can ask a favor." She dropped her head in her hands. A spiny knot of disappointment scratched at the back of her throat every time she swallowed. "You need to go out there and pacify the people who made the trip today."

"How do you expect me to do that?"

There had to be something here they could use to get control of the situation. The organized desk held pen and paper. She tapped her chin, discarding a couple of ideas before settling on one. If they gave the guests something free for their inconvenience, they might be able to salvage the day.

She thrust the items into Ash's hands. "Explain the delay in the delivery. In the meantime, we're giving them a voucher for a free dessert at the diner."

"I'm not normally like this, Quinn. I'm sorry."

She studied him a long time. Glimpses of a dependable man flashed in those golden eyes, but he quickly donned his mask of indifference. "Sure. Go take care of our guests."

She pulled out her phone and scrolled through her list of contacts until she found the one she wanted. She pushed the call symbol and waited for the ring. "Rocky, hi. Quinn McAllister."

It took twenty minutes, the promise of another large order in the middle of the month, and one coffee date with the owner's son, but the trees would arrive in two hours.

Quinn searched out Jim to give him the good news and found him out by the Santa tent.

"What happened?" Her manager asked.

"Good news, they'll be in here in two hours. Bad news, I have to meet Rocky for coffee after the holidays."

"You've avoided that for over a year. I guess he got to you."

Jim shuffled from one foot to the other and ran his finger under his collar.

"What's up? It looks like you have something to say." Quinn patted him on the shoulder.

"What about him? He needs to go."

She didn't need to ask who *he* referred to. "There isn't a lot we can do. Henri demanded he stay. We have no choice, we have to figure out how to make this work. But one thing is certain, we have to show him what a wonderful place this is. How friendly everyone is. Somehow, we need to convince him there is a reason to hold on to their ownership. We have to be nice."

That meant her too. She needed to figure out a way to turn things around. If Ash was treated like an outsider, he had no reason to keep their inheritance. They'd make way more money in the sale. Even if they did only sell their half. "I'm going to find Ash and head back to the house. Good luck here."

"Thanks. I'll let you know how it goes." Jim waved her off, already involved with the crowd.

She found Ash by the Santa tent passing out vouchers. She motioned him away from the ears of the people in line.

"What happened?"

"It's all fixed. I need you here with Jim. Once we have them, help unload and get them where they need to be. You can assist with crowd control in the meantime. Keep people happy. Some people drive here from a distance and might get pretty upset. Keep handing out those vouchers and send them over to Amy at the restaurant."

"Do you think this is the best place for me? I don't think Christmas sales are my strength."

"Ash, you are irresponsible. Self-centered, and I would hazard a guess, self-destructive. This town's livelihood depends on us, and the business we draw." She bit off the rest of the sharp speech. *Nice. She would turn this around.* Softening her expression, she continued. "I understand you don't want to be here. I'm sorry Henri forced this on you. Believe me, I wish I understood why. But here we are. You created this mess. You can help clean it up. I'll figure where to put you next."

She zipped her coat, pulled her furry hood around her face, and turned into the wind. The cold would help clear her head.

Ash's gaze followed Quinn up the street until she turned the corner out of sight. He wiped his hand over his face.

One job. Order the trees, and he couldn't even do that. He hated the disappointment on Jim and Quinn's face. Years ago, when he learned nothing he did would make his father happy, he'd changed tactics. He'd quit trying. If you were always going to be called out for something, why go the extra mile?

But these people were not his father, and he let them down. She was right. He was behaving childishly. There had to be a way he could make it up. To both of them.

Chapter Ten

A sh smiled at the last child to come off Santa's lap. She beamed back at him as he handed her a candy cane. It had been the elf's job, but she had to leave.

Since his screw-up was the reason they were shorthanded, it seemed only fair he step in and help. It meant he'd been out in the cold most of the day. Even with borrowed gloves, he was a freeze-pop. The kind his grandmother used to give him when he came out of the pool. *Now, where did that come from?* He hadn't thought of those summer days in years. The days when his father dropped him and Eric at their grandparents were the best because it had meant freedom. He pushed away the memory.

"That's a wrap, Santa," he said to the big guy in the red suit.

"Outstanding job, young fella. I'd say you'll make the nice list this year," Santa replied as they both headed out of the tent.

"I don't know about that. You must have missed the *how Ash ruined Christmas* saga."

"Yeah, I heard."

Ash gave a dry laugh. "Pardon me, Santa, but if you know, I'm not sure how you could put me on the nice list."

The man placed a hand on Ash's shoulder. "Son, Santa may have a different scale he judges by. It's not the mistakes we make in life that define us. How do we rise to the occasion? You stepped up to the plate. It's possible Santa's helpers noticed. Have a good night."

"Night, Santa."

Ash headed for the store to close up. Jim had needed to leave early and surprised Ash when he asked him to close. There wasn't a snowball's chance in west Texas he would mess this up.

He double-checked all the doors were locked and did one more walk-through to make sure no one hid inside. He still reeled from his blunder of the tree order and tried to come up with a way to make it all right.

In the long run, none of it mattered. He and Eric intended to sell, and, if Quinn was right, the resort had no desire to continue with all these silly traditions and sentimental emotions. No doubt Quinn would fight them, but they would wear her down.

His current behavior would not earn him points with Quinn. He'd need to channel his inner Christmas spirit.

The tree day opener was a huge deal to the shop and the town. Families came for Santa, to have lunch, pick out their tree, and spend the day Christmas shopping. They dumped money into the economy.

His chest tightened. That he let Quinn and everyone else down, didn't sit well with him.

He stopped at the front door and switched off the lights.

On the way to drop Eric off at the airport, the two of them discussed Henri's endgame. There had to be a reason why she kept Ash in Elf Hollow. She had an agenda, they needed to figure out what it was. Best guess, it was a delay tactic. Postpone the inevitable sale. Give Quinn enough time to change his mind.

They'd underestimated his need for cash.

Something Jim had said the other day bothered him. Henri hoped he'd find something here. Other than brutal temperatures and the annoyance of holiday festivities, there wasn't much to hold onto.

Quinn and her caramel-colored hair taunted him. "I wish I knew what you're up to Aunt Henri. 'Cause I'm a fish out of water up here, and the sooner I get this placed sold, the quicker I can get home." *You would've been better off to leave it all to Quinn.*

He stepped into the night air, the wind whisking his breath away. Did it ever stop? The cold seeped into his bones. What he wouldn't give for ten minutes under the Houston sun.

Floodlights lit the sidewalk outside the B&B, where Quinn shoveled snow from the path, her goofy dog hopping through the mounds. The glow from the streetlamp caught snowflake sprinkles dotted on caramel strands that peeked out from under her knit hat.

He stopped, spellbound. Smooth and methodical in her movements, Quinn made the mundane task graceful and effortless. As she threw a shovelful of snow to the side, Niko pounced, and her laughter carried on the night air.

A pulse, quick and hard pounded in his throat. The power of the moment caught him off guard with its simplicity, the delight Quinn brought to an otherwise desolate scene.

Christmas lights illuminated the porch in reds, greens, and blues, the silence a blanket over the night. His focus shifted. Rather than a bleak landscape, the raw beauty of winter showed itself. He would never think of winter and not remember Quinn.

"It's ten o'clock. Don't you ever stop?" He shouted.

She glanced up mid-shovel and then tossed the snow into the pile on the side of the walk. "Never. As long as there is work to do, someone's got to do it. How did things go?" She didn't take the time to stop and chat but kept on working. "I came by earlier to check in on things. Jim said you did a terrific job with the kids."

"I never realized how much fun the Christmas-monsters could be all hyped up on candy canes and stoked to see Santa." He couldn't remember one trip to see Santa. "Everything worked out. People left with smiles on their faces. Again, I'm sorry for how that played out."

"I am too." She tossed another load of snow before he could reach her.

"Here. Let me do that." He took the shovel from her hands before she could protest. "I've never shoveled snow. This should be interesting."

"Well, since you put it like that."

Five minutes later, his breathing reached workout level, and the snow came down almost faster than he could remove it. He turned. Quinn sat on the cleared sidewalk, Niko at her side. He tipped his head back and stared at the star-studded black sky. "You do this every day? I'd rather have icicles shoved under my nails than do this another minute."

"It would be easier if you dressed right. No hat, thin leather gloves, no scarf, and don't get me started on the itty-bitty windbreaker that couldn't."

"Hey, now. Don't be dissing this sexy beauty. Its gotten me through many Texas winters." He leaned on the shovel and plucked at the collar. "I'll admit it's not standing up to the Minnesota stuff you got up here. Then again, in my defense, I'm supposed to be back home in warm Houston right now."

She shrugged. "Why don't you buy something more? You'd be much happier. I promise." She stretched out on the sidewalk already coated with more snow and waved her arms and legs back and forth. "See, I'm making snow angels and I'm warm as toast."

He picked up a shovelful of snow and dropped it on her. "That should cool you off."

Her squeal piqued his competitive nature, and he picked up more. But the minute he turned around, a snowball slammed him in the face.

He threw the shovel on the ground and rubbed his hands together. "You're on, sister." Among the bellows of laughter, Niko barked and ran from one to the other determined to catch a mouthful of snow. In the flicker of Christmas lights from the porch, his mind cleared, and lightness floated through his limbs. Joy. And for the first time, the idea of Christmas didn't fill him with dread.

They went on like that for another twenty minutes until Niko jumped at the same time Quinn stepped. She fell right into Ash's arms. He landed in a soft pile of snow, Quinn snuggled in the crook of his arm, body sprawled over him. Her face, rosy with cold and laughter, hovered above his. Lips, ruby red and plump, were a kiss away. Inches separated him from the sweetness he wanted to taste.

With reluctance, he rolled to the side and stood before he pulled her from the ground. "I call a truce. I'm too cold to go on."

She brushed the snow off his shoulder. "You'll get frostbite out here. Tomorrow, you need to get something warmer."

"I haven't found anything at the few stores around here."

"They have a bigger selection over in Grand Marais. You should go there."

A plan formed. "I should. You should go with me."

"No, no—"

"Yes. Yes, you can, and you will. I have no clue where to go, and the rental car doesn't have GPS."

The wheels turned in that active, brilliant mind as she

worked to come up with what he would bet was an excuse. "Wouldn't Henri want you to show me around the area?"

"Fine. We'll go tomorrow afternoon. We have guests arriving in the morning. Kylee won't be here until eleven. It's the only time I have free, and we need to find something for you soon." She turned her gaze to the night sky, where the snow swirled. "Come on. That's enough. It's coming down harder. At this point, it's hitting the ground faster than you can clear it."

"Are you coming inside or going back to your place?"

"Mine. The guests are settled, and I'm officially off duty."

"I'll go with you."

"Thanks for your help." Her voice soft, almost shy.

"I didn't do much, but you're welcome."

He took her elbow as they followed the path to the back of the house. His lips burned from the imagined kiss. His chest tightened. Goosebumps spread across his skin that had nothing to do with the temperature. His fingers itched to trace the lines of her face.

No. No, no. He reeled his thoughts in before they took on a mind of their own, and a shiver rippled through him. His wet clothes stuck to places they had no business sticking.

"Have you thought anymore about what you want to do at the end of this month?"

She glanced at him from the side then turned her attention to the icy path. "Have you? Have you forgotten we can't discuss that?"

"Just curious what your thoughts were."

She came to an abrupt halt and pivoted, feet sliding for purchase. "My plans haven't changed. I suspect neither have yours." Those lips made of daydreams curled into a brilliant smile. "But, the month is still young."

They slid the last few feet to her cottage and stopped at her step.

He blew on his cupped hands. "Here we are."

"Yup. Here we are."

"What's the plan for the morning?"

"It's Sunday, sleep in. We'll leave around noon."

"Do you take Sundays off?"

"Not with a house full of guests. But I should be able to get out for the afternoon. Goodnight, Ash."

"Good night, Quinn."

She stared up at him, silky strands tossed about in the wind. She opened her mouth as if to say something but smiled instead and walked inside.

He waved goodnight, his heart knocking against his ribs. It was increasingly difficult to ignore his growing fondness of her. She was nothing like the quirky, shallow women in his past. Throwing money at her would not make her happy, quite the opposite to be sure. She didn't thumb her nose at convention or want to explore her rebellious side.

He reversed his steps and headed back to the warmth of the main house. Quinn was beautiful, hardworking, and loyal to a fault. All the qualities he'd spent a lifetime trying to avoid.

So, why did his heart, a hardened lump of clay, long dead, surge with a renewed sense of energy?

Chapter Eleven

A sh held the door open for Quinn and waved her under
his arm. "After you."

She stumbled through the threshold, laughter pinching
her sides. "Seriously, this is the last store you can go to. It's the
only semi-mega sports store around. If you can't find something here, you're not going too. Besides, I'm getting faint
from all this running around."

"Ah, quit your whining, we had a hearty lunch."

"Yea, two hours and four miles ago. We've been walking all
over this town. You're pickier than any woman I know."

"I believe the word you're looking for is... particular. I
know what I like."

She snickered, the muscles of her cheeks achy from the
constant smile she wore. They'd left Elf Hollow around noon
and pulled into Grand Marais in time for lunch. Fun and easy
to talk to, Ash put her at ease. She couldn't remember the last
time she was this relaxed. The knotted burrs lodged between
her shoulder blades dissolved thirty minutes into lunch.

"What about this one?" She pulled a hanger off the clear-
ance rack. "It's a nice gray, not too thick, Thinsulate, and it's

only fifty dollars." She held it beneath her chin and shuffled her feet. "It appears to meet your impossible standards."

"Not impossible. High. I have *high* standards. Let me see that." He took the hanger from her and rubbed the material, checked the zipper, and flipped the hood. "I don't do hoods."

"You don't do hoods. K." She hung it back on the rack. "I get it. They rub the neck—"

"It blocks my view." He walked to a full-price display and pulled a similar coat off its hanger. "This has promise. Thin, says it's Thinsulate, nice zipper, most importantly, no hood."

She held up the price tag and about choked. "And two hundred fifty dollars! You must be insane."

"You get what you pay for. Here, hold this." He shrugged out of his windbreaker and handed it to her. Sliding the new coat off the hanger, he examined it in great detail before he put it on, zipped it, flexed his arms, and swung them like an air traffic controller. "What? Why are you laughing?"

"I can't help it. You look like you're flagging a plane into the gate."

"For your information, this is how you test for quality."

"Huh. And direct a plane into the gate."

He walked to a mirror and checked his image before swiveling to face her. "What do you think?"

The hairs along her arms swayed and tickled. She swallowed the first words to come to mind. She didn't think *sexy, or hottie* had much to do with the purchase of a winter jacket.

"It's nice. As nice as that one over there for two hundred dollars less."

"I like this. Now I need a hat and gloves."

"And a scarf. Don't forget a scarf."

His cocky, masculine grin sent fragile bubbles of joy dancing up from her core.

"Do real men wear scarves?"

She shrugged and dropped one shoulder. "They do if they want to stay warm."

"There are better ways to get warm."

She grabbed the fabric of the coat. "Come on."

"Lead the way."

She dropped his arm, so he could remove the coat. "It looks like you'll have your pick of styles." Quinn pulled a hat off the rack and swirled to show him the prize, but he was nowhere in sight. "Ash? For goodness' sake, you're like a child. Where are you?" She wandered down another aisle.

"Over here. Follow my voice. I can whistle if you'd like."

"No! Keep talking. I'll find you."

"You have no idea what you're missing. I can carry a tune."

"See? I told you'd I'd find you. What are you doing over here? You were looking for hats." She picked up a package. "Long underwear?"

"I told you there were other ways to stay warm."

Her mouth dropped open.

"What did you think I meant?" He tapped her on the chin. "Get your mind out of the gutter, darlin'."

"Quinn?" A hand tapped her shoulder to get her attention.

She spun around. The brain worked to process the person who stood in front of her. But the heart already thumped in recognition like a jackrabbit. "Erin. What... what are you doing here?" Was this for real? Vertigo made her head swim, and she choked in large gulps of air to ease the nausea that rolled in her stomach.

"I thought that was you." The young woman hugged Quinn and stepped back. Her gaze roamed over Ash.

"Erin, what are you doing here? Last I saw you, you were in St. Paul." *Shacking up with Ty.*

"About all that. I'm sorry how that all played out. I made

some bad choices back then. Learned my lesson, I tell ya. Ty is a real piece of work. But I've changed."

"Yeah. Sure. What are you doing in Grand Marais? Do you live here now?" Please, no. The idea of this woman in her backyard was unthinkable.

"No, visiting. Some friends have a cabin up here." She raked her gaze over Ash. "Who's your friend?" Her voice turned husky, and she held out her hand to him. "I'm a friend of Quinn's from college. You must be her boyfriend?"

A grunt slipped past Quinn's lips. She would never count boyfriend-stealing Erin as a friend. "Ash is my... business partner. Ash, this is Erin Simmons."

He held out his hand. "Hello."

Erin now stood between Quinn and Ash with her back to Quinn.

Changed my ass. "Okay. Well, it's been fun taking this trip down memory lane with you, but we need to go. Ash, let's go pay for that coat." She grabbed a pair of gloves off the rack, shoved them in his hand, and forced a grimace at Erin. "Nice seeing you again, have a great time here. It's a fun town."

"What was that all about?" Ash leaned down and whispered in her ear.

"For the love of all that is holy, keep walking. Whatever you do, don't look back."

The line to pay was five people deep. Quinn fidgeted from foot to foot, a million bitsy ants tingling over her skin.

He paid, and she dodged out the door to scratch the imaginary devils off her. "Of all the people to run into—"

"Who was that?"

"Someone who annoys me to no end."

"I see that, but you don't want *her* to see that." His gaze scanned the street before he tucked her hand under his arm. "Come on. I know the perfect thing." He guided her away from the store to the coffee shop at the end of the street. The bell gave a cheerful chime as they entered and found a booth.

"You're shivering. Coffee should do the trick. You sit here, and I'll get us both a cup."

Less than five minutes later, he came back with two paper cups, steaming with the scent of coffee.

"You're a lifesaver." She stood and took the promised elixir.

"Where are you going?"

"To get creamer and sugar."

"I already hooked you up."

She gave the cup, and him, a skeptical stare. "Not to sound like a sugar fiend, but I have a precise mixture. I'm gonna go doctor it up." She pointed her thumbs at the coffee bar.

"Aren't you going to taste it first?"

"No offense, but no one gets it right. Not even people who've known me forever, and you expect me to trust you have it figured out in under two weeks?"

He leaned against the seat back and crossed his arms, an *ain't I clever* expression plastered on his face. "Go ahead. I dare you."

"You seem pretty sure of yourself," She raised an eyebrow and sat down.

"How about a wager?"

She pinned him with a stare of amusement. "What did you have in mind?" Probably not a good idea to bet a man with a Cheshire-cat grin, but she liked the rush of adrenaline that came from an occasional walk on the wild side.

"If I win, you tell me what that captivating flashback in the store was all about."

"And if I win?"

He thought about it a minute and shrugged a shoulder. "You have one question."

She chewed her lip. On the one hand, she didn't want to

UNDER A CHRISTMAS MOON

expose her dirty laundry, but she *did* like the odds. How could she lose? Even after they'd lived together for a year. Ty had no clue how she took her coffee. "You're on." She raised the cup to her lips.

He put his hand on her forearm. "You have to be honest with your answer. You can't pretend. No tricks. Agreed?"

"Agreed." She brought the steaming cup to her lips and took a sip. Her eyebrow cocked in surprise. *Impossible.*

"I knew it. You don't have to say a word. I can tell by the pure joy written on your face. I did good, didn't I?"

"Gloating is not becoming on anyone."

"Yeah, yeah. Spill it." He settled into the booth and waited for her to start.

If the floor opened right now, she would jump in head-first. Why was it so hard to confess the deepest, darkest parts of your life? She rubbed the temples that throbbed in time to the new age music that spilled from the speakers. "Can you face that direction?" She waved at the other side of the room.

"What?"

"Over there. Turn your head that way." She waved her hand in the vague direction of the wood-paneled wall.

He turned on the bench and stretched his legs on the seat. Gaze straight ahead. "Is this better?"

"No. Yes, it's fine. I'm going to start. Right here." She chewed on her bottom lip fingers fiddling with the cardboard coffee sleeve. Who said she had to tell him everything? No emotions, nothing but the facts. "I dated Ty in college. It was more than dating, at least that's what I thought. We lived together for almost a year. We met in my freshman year and we... clicked. He made me laugh, he was sexy, and he oozed confidence. That was attractive to misfit Quinn, and he took me under his wing." She took a breather and a sip of the hot liquid for strength.

"Is that when you moved in together? Freshman year?"

"No. That didn't happen until we came back from summer break. It seemed like the natural progression."

"Did you see him over the summer?" He turned his head in her direction.

"No peeking, buster. And no, we didn't see each other. I lived up here, and he's from Iowa. But we did all the things couples do long distance. It wasn't until we started our sophomore year things went south." She was too blind to see it for what it was.

She examined the words on the molded lid as if they held the key to unlock all the mysteries of the world. "He screwed up and lost his student housing, the roommate he lined up bailed, and he moved in with me. It was great. At first. It didn't take long before he missed dates, dinners, and lied about it. My friends tried to tell me he was using me, but I ignored them. When we were together, he made me feel like I was the most special person in the world. That he couldn't live without me." Why not say, *I'm a pathetic loser* and move on?

"Quinn, you don't have to keep going. I'm sorry I made you dredge it all up."

"Don't do that," she snapped. "Geez, this is hard enough without your pity."

"That wasn't pity. It was empathy. There's a difference."

She found it very hard to believe anyone would cheat on him.

"I know what it feels like to want someone to care about you. Like you would do almost anything to get their approval." Ash's voice dropped to a hoarse whisper, and the lightness of their afternoon together turned heavy. "Can I turn around now?"

"No."

"I promise to behave."

"Fine. But don't make this anymore awkward than it already is."

He righted himself in the booth. His hand made it halfway across the table before he stopped and jerked it back.

"I came home from a study group one night to find him with Erin. I left that night, and I never went back."

"Where did you go?"

"I moved in with a friend. There were only two months left in the year. I came home and finished my degree online."

She'd hated herself for that cowardice move. It had taken her a long time to put it all behind her. She'd sooner lose a kidney than allow a man to play her like that again.

Ash drummed the tips of his fingers on the table, puffed up his cheeks, and blew out the air. "Once when I was twelve, my best friend, Nick, had our first boy-girl party. We were excited. And I invited this girl, Natalie Lee. Prettiest girl in school."

"You were twelve?" Was he seriously comparing her break-up with Ty, to this?

A half-grin settled on his mouth. "Natalie was *my* girl. Well, at least in my twelve-year-old head she was. About halfway through the party, I couldn't find Nick or Natalie. I went looking, and there they were, in the backyard, Nick, with his lips on her cheek." He shook his head. "Broke my heart forever."

She stared, fascinated, as he tried to keep the serious expression. As he struggled to keep the muscles around his mouth and jaw from twitching.

"You're pulling my leg."

Crinkles edged his eyes. "Trying to make you laugh. Did it work?"

It did. The heaviness in her chest eased. She could breathe deep for the first time since Erin called out her name back in the store. "Did any of that really happen?"

He shrugged and blinked. "It was not a party. It was in the

game store. It wasn't a girl. It was the latest hot video game. He got it. I didn't. Same thing, right?"

Her laughter drew the attention of the other coffee drinkers, but she didn't care. It wasn't what he said that was particularly funny. It was the intent behind the words. She took a sip of her perfectly made coffee. Maybe Ash Larsen had more layers than she first thought.

On the way home, Ash glanced from the road to the petite woman beside him.

As she'd talked about this Ty jerk, it was all he could do not to run and hide. Her words were a truth he didn't want to hear. At some point in his life, he'd been someone's Ty.

Making her laugh had been the only thing he could think to do.

He slid another long, side glance at the woman who was turning his life upside down. She deserved more.

Chapter Twelve

"What's going on there? It sounds like you're at a party."

Ash rose from the chair in the living room and walked into the dim entryway. "Not a party, a snowstorm. There's a blizzard blowing out there. The power is out, and everyone is huddled in the living room in front of the fire." Well, almost everyone.

Despite the lack of heat, Quinn circled the perimeter of the room and asked someone to blow out a candle then replaced it with a lantern. A stray hair fell over her eye, and she tucked it behind her ear. Three days since their outing to Grand Marais. Three days since something inside changed. He couldn't put his finger on what exactly.

"Dude, blizzards are no joke."

"Can't be worse than hurricanes."

"Snowdrifts higher than cars, line the street, and it's blowing around so much I couldn't even see Quinn's cottage."

"You can keep it. It's eighty and sunny here today." Eric's tone was smug.

A couple of kids pulled a box off the bookshelves. Others

gathered around a table where they dumped the contents. Quinn brought them another lantern and a bowl of potato chips.

Ash's phone buzzed in his ear, and his watch showed a text message from Thomas, his contact on the restaurant lease. "Hold up. I'm getting a text." He flicked the text message to the front of his screen. *Great news. Business is slow with the holidays. They've agreed to extend your application for the lease on the restaurant space until the end of January. It's a go, baby!* His heart thundered in his ears. *Yes!* That was the best news he'd received in weeks.

"Hello? I don't have all night. You gonna give me an update or what? The fam is waiting to go to dinner." Eric's brisk voice broke through Ash's musings.

"Right. No update."

"What? What are you doing there?"

Screwing things up. "Working. Learning what I can. Like Henri wanted."

"Okay. I would have thought you'd have gone another way with your time."

"It's a different world up here, Eric. There's no subterfuge. You know where you stand with these people. They leave their doors unlocked and keys in their cars."

"Even with the resort traffic?"

"Yup. Maybe not on the Main Street, but you get the idea."

He took a chair in the corner with a view into the living room. Quinn passed from one guest to another laughing, touching a shoulder here, pulling a blanket higher for another.

An older couple, the McCrays, if he remembered correctly, and two families all arrived within the last few days. Another family had been due that morning, but the storm kept them away.

"It's different here at the B&B. There's life here. Right

now, there are two families with two kids each. They'll both be here until New Year's Day. There is an older couple who will be here all month as well. Quinn has activities planned for all of them."

His brother's chuckle came through loud and clear. "It must be killing you. What are you doing for nightlife? I can see the appeal the resort has for people."

"Yes, but if we sell to them, the lodge, they'll tear it all down. Their only interest is in the lakefront status. What happens to the people who come for peace and quiet?" Ash puffed out a breath and rubbed a finger down the bridge of his nose. How did this become so complicated? Sell the property. Take the money, leave oil company, start a restaurant. He should already be home making plans.

"*If* we sell? When did it become a question?" Eric asked.

"All I'm suggesting is maybe we look for another buyer. Quinn might be more open to the sale if they didn't want to tear it down." At least he hoped she'd feel that way.

Eric grunted. "It's all about location. The ski resort wants it, and they have the ability to pay for it. Although I honestly don't know if they would only buy half."

That's the last thing he wanted. They'd make life difficult for her until she caved. And he'd gotten to know Quinn well enough now, she wouldn't go down without a fight.

"Look, I need to go. I don't want to wear down my battery any more than it is."

"Hold up. I gotta other news. I don't think you're going to have a job much longer. Dad is madder than I've ever seen him over Jackson-gate."

"Jackson-gate?"

"That's what they're calling it in HR. But he's mad."

"Won't be the first time."

"No. But it may be the last time."

"That bad, huh?" He couldn't hide the disappointment in

his voice. Ash's father had been threatening to fire him for years, but he'd never had the ammunition before.

"Why didn't you fire the guy like he told you to? Do you get enjoyment in rocking the boat and pissing him off?"

Ash sighed and stretched his legs out in front of him. He'd spent years trying to earn his father's approval. But that horse done left the barn a long time ago.

Quinn's laugh floated in from the other room. She was unruffled by the chaos the blizzard caused as it raged outside. Confident. How ironic the freshman Quinn sought someone with self-assurance when that quiet characteristic lie within her.

"I'm sorry, Ash. I gotta go, Lizzy's getting antsy for dinner. I'll talk to you in a few days. Think about what I said." Eric hung up before Ash could reply.

He stuffed his phone in his pocket and turned his attention to the occupants of the room.

Quinn caught his eye. Warmth spread through him as she glided across the darkened room toward him.

"Hi, you got a minute? I wanted to show you something." She pulled a crinkled envelope, yellowed from age, from her front pocket. "Remember the box of letters the attorney gave us?"

He nodded.

She handed him the envelope. "I think you should read this. From what I can tell, it's the first letter Sadie wrote Henri. It clears up the mystery of what happened all those years ago." She turned to walk away, but then she did the most outrageous thing. She came back and kissed his forehead.

It was chaste, and sweet, and meant to be comforting, but the hum of anticipation thrummed through his body. The sway of her hips as she walked away was hypnotic, and he drank in every step like a man dying of thirst.

She took a seat against the doorway furthest from the fireplace, releasing him from his trance. He turned to the letter.

My dearest Henny-Penny (I hope I may still call you that)

After five years, I'm sure you never thought to hear from me again.

And maybe you won't welcome this letter. If I don't hear back from you,

I will take that as your answer to leave you in peace. Something you greatly

deserve. But many things have changed, and I feel the need to clean the air.

I guess having a child does that to you.

Yes, I am a mother. My son, Joe, is three months old. Every day I look at him

and I think of what I lost to be where I am today. And you, my sweet sister,

were that sacrifice. The one person who always loved me, no matter my wild

ways. The one person who defended me daily and took care of me.

Ash stopped, trying to picture his prim, proper, grandmother, the personification of the southern belle, wild and uncontrollable. It didn't fit.

Please, don't be angry at Travis. The fault lies squarely with me. You see,

I tricked him one night all those years ago. It was after your fight. You

remember, the battle over your wedding date? You were so upset. I went

to him to offer comfort. In the dark, he thought I was you. And to my shame,

I let him. By the time he figured it out in the light of morning, it was too late.

The deed was done, and neither of us could turn back time.

A few months later, when I discovered I was pregnant, we did what, at the time,

seemed like the right thing. I see now it was the coward's way. To leave you and

mother and father to deal with the scandal I'm sure ensued. Travis has never

forgiven me for that night.

We settled in a town in Texas, and Travis found a job with an oil company. He

works as a roughneck and is gone for weeks at a time. We lost the baby a month

after we were married. I hope this letter has found you with a new love and a

new life, and even though I don't deserve forgiveness, I hope you have enough

love left in your heart to do that.

With love,

Sadie

He read it through twice before it all sank in. It shocked him to think of his grandmother as *the other woman.* Poor Henri. He didn't blame her for not forgiving them. But it did explain a lot.

He never felt much emotion between his grandparents. All the more reason to doubt love existed. His grandfather didn't love Henri enough to face her and work things through. He didn't love his grandmother enough to forgive her one indiscretion, and his father couldn't forgive him for the death of his mother. Maybe it was only his messed-up family that had issues.

The evening came to an end. Exhausted kids piled together in front of the fireplace, surrounded by blankets and pillows. Adults all snuggled under their own quilts. The soft glow of the lantern and Christmas tree lights washed over them all.

There was a raging snowstorm blowing outside the walls, and yet the occupants shared a togetherness akin to family. Something clicked, a piece of the puzzle he didn't know he'd been building.

He stood and grabbed a blanket as he walked into the room.

He nudged Quinn's leg and nodded for her to move over.

She scooted far enough over to give him some wall space. He sat down next to her and pulled her into the crook of his arm.

She pulled away, "What are you doing?"

"Conserving body heat. Don't argue with me." He settled the blanket over them both and pulled the end up under her chin. She hesitated no more than a breath and then rested her head on his shoulders.

Bundled as they were together under the blanket, it wasn't hard to imagine the kind of marriage Eric talked about. The idea was foreign to him. The top of her head, nestled between his shoulder and chest. She made it very clear the other day the stable kinda guy she wanted in her life. He was not that person. Would never be that person.

Quinn deserved to be loved and cherished.

Chapter Thirteen

Quinn tucked the last of the supplies into the food basket and grabbed a few extra blankets. It was their first Saturday S'mores by the Lake of the season. She'd had Barney set up the chairs and fire pit an hour ago. There should be plenty of heat in the area. The other supplies would already be there waiting for the kids.

She was thrilled the party was still a go. When the blizzard blew through the middle of the week, it dropped over three feet of snow over two days. She hadn't been sure if they would have enough time to get the area cleared, but she'd called in extra help, and they were up and running.

She had a sneaking suspicion Ash never experienced a s'mores party. At least not the winter kind. Humming to herself, she put the large basket of supplies by the back door and went in search of the man that took up way too much of her thoughts. He was different. She couldn't put her finger on it, but ever since the tree fiasco, he'd changed. Seemed more engaged with the activities and the people.

Ash came down the stairs as she strolled into the lobby. He

even carried himself different. The stress lines were gone. His lips were relaxed, softer, one could even say, pillowy lips. *No, one would not say that. Geez.*

"I was coming to find you," she said with a breathless tone.

"You found me. I was looking for you, too. Wanna grab a late lunch?"

"Nope, but get your winter gear and meet me in the kitchen. We have some business to handle."

"Be right back."

She slipped into her own coat and scarf before she pushed her feet into Sorrel boots. She was pulling her gloves on when Ash came back, decked out in his new winter clothes.

"You look nice and warm."

"It's colder than a well-digger's knees out there. I better be warm."

"It's what?" A laughed busted from her before she could stop it.

"My family may not have originated in Texas, but my father was born and raised there, and I spend a lot of time in the oilfields. The roughnecks I come in contact with have a very colorful way of making a point."

"Real winter awaits us. Trust me, you're going to be even happier with your gear when you see where we're going." She picked up the blankets. "Grab the basket and let's go."

She led the way out the kitchen door. The scents in the air, sharp and brittle with cold, slapped them in the face, surrounded her with love for the season. Her laughter danced along on the icy breeze. She would never tire of the beauty of winter. "Be careful, salt doesn't work well when it gets this cold. There are icy patches."

"What are we doing with all this? Looks like fixins' for s'mores."

"That would be correct."

"Isn't that a campfire kinda activity?"

She shook her head. "And how do you think we're going to keep warm? Be careful through here. It's not a real path." She took him off the cobblestone and through a stand of trees. The pinewood scent from the fire pit hit them seconds before the flames came into view when they emerged from the trees. For the longest time, she couldn't stand the smell. But eventually, she came to tolerate it. Flames... she didn't think she'd ever get over them.

Three families with kids sat huddled together.

"When did the other family get here?" Ash asked.

"Late last night. They said the roads were good for the most part all the way in. The state MDOT is pretty good at getting them cleared quickly."

As cold as it was, the McCrays opted for the great indoors. She couldn't blame them. The idea of being inside where the warmth spread into the bones sounded mighty good. Curled up reading a great book. Who was she kidding? She'd be bored within five minutes.

Ash didn't wait to be told what to do but jumped right into the fray. His voice boomed, high-fiving with the kids, he emanated energy as he pulled stakes from the basket. "Who's ready for s'mores?"

"Me!" the kids all chorused together.

Barney helped him pass out the marshmallows and supervise.

"Hey, Quinn, the adult s'mores hot chocolate was a nice touch," Carly Dawson said.

"You're new here, but these are a highlight all month long," Gemma Nelson answered as she waved the Styrofoam cup. "We've been coming here for the last three years, and I think this is my favorite part."

"Glad you like them. I don't know how long we'll be out here in these temperatures. But steamy drinks always help. We have more when you are ready. Everyone have enough blankets? We brought a few more." Quinn passed them around and made sure everyone had what they needed before she settled herself.

She took the bench as far from the flames as possible, but where she could still feel the heat. She toothed off a glove and pulled out her phone.

Earlier, Barney had placed a few Bluetooth speakers in the area. All she needed to do was start her playlist. Christmas music blared filling the air, eliciting cheers from all the sticky-faced kids. She draped a blanket over her lap and sat back to enjoy the scene.

It played out as she imagined with couples huddled together on the two-seater benches, heads bent together in laughter or talking, and kids singing along to the songs.

Ash was a big kid himself, bouncing from child to child to make sure they were all set and knew how to toast their marshmallow. As someone would shout, "Done," he would bring them a square of chocolate and two graham crackers. As soon as they ate one, he would load them up for another. Every now and then, he'd peer over at her, and his relaxed easy manner made her heart flutter.

She loved seeing him have this fun. After she'd given him the letter from Sadie, she'd been worried he'd be upset. Learning his grandmother broke up her sister and fiancé had to be difficult, but he took it in stride. Sadie shared her life in those letters, but Henri's story unfolded as well in the scribbled script.

A young girl shyly handed her a s'mores. "Mr. Ash said to bring this to you."

"Aren't you sweet? Tell *Mr.* Ash, thank you." Their gazes clashed across the fire, and she raised an eyebrow. *Thank you.* She mouthed.

She chatted with the new couple getting to know them

better. They'd been referred by some friends in the Twin Cities, they were only there for a week and planned to Christmas shop before they headed home.

The cold didn't seem to bother anyone as the next time Quinn checked at her watch, nearly an hour and a half had passed. She always knew where to find him. The few times he caught her attention, he motioned her over to the pit with a loaded skewer. There wasn't enough chocolate on the planet to entice her anywhere near that inferno. Ice water, colder than the air, ran in her veins at the mere thought.

The stronger side of her wished she could put the past behind her and let it all go, but Henri and Emerson, the town, made it easy for her to cling to her fears. Catered to her determination to hold onto the past. She'd been carrying it for so long she didn't know what to do with it. How does one unpack a fear that is as much a part of you as the hair on your head?

Ash took the seat next to her and pulled a corner of the blanket over his legs. He passed her a creamy s'more.

"Since you won't come to the s'mores, I'll keep bringing them to you."

She took a bite of the warm gooey goodness. "Oh my gosh, that's good."

"Why don't you make one with me?"

Families began to cry *uncle* and pack up the kids.

"You've got to be freezing. Let me move the chair closer—"

"No." Her voice sounded much harsher than she intended. She swallowed and tried again. "I'm fine. Besides, I think things are winding down."

His gaze scrutinized her until she squirmed in her seat.

"I don't buy that. Ever since I got here, I've watched you skirt flames no matter how small."

She lowered her lashes and glanced away. The man may be a player, but he didn't miss a thing. He figured out her coffee when no one else had, and most people didn't pay enough attention to recognize she avoided flames. After all these years, her friends accepted it as a quirk.

She dropped the blanket onto his lap. "It looks like the party is over." Everyone drifted up the path, and Barney extinguished the fire. Her cue to round everything up.

Ash followed, gathering blankets and folding them into a neat pile. She tracked him out of the corner of her eye. Smooth, confident, self-assured. So much like Ty, yet so different.

Ty would never have let that go. He would have badgered her to tears. Had done that, and then once he found out her secret, he relished every opportunity to tease her for her *weakness* as he called it. When the terror choked her, he would apologize profusely and tell her to take it easy. He only wanted to help. Deep down, she knew her fear embarrassed him. She refused to go to the bonfires on campus and at the lakes.

"You ready? Winter coat or not, I don't think I can take another second of this cold." His reassuring grin made her heart pound. Every muscle of her body quivered.

Was it possible she could actually trust him?

Hours later, Ash turned off the lights, flicked on the fire, and crawled in bed. Another day spent with Quinn that ended with a grin wider than the Rio Grande.

The more time they spent together, the more he wanted to know *her*. What made her tick? Not only how she took her coffee, but her favorite food, movies she liked, how she spent her days off.

And why she avoided fire.

He pulled the blankets higher, and in that space between awake and dreaming they met. And nothing stood between them.

Chapter Fourteen

"Have a good night." Ash waved at the last customer and locked the door behind them. An hour earlier, Amy boasted they'd been busy for a Sunday. Which didn't say much. He'd come in at noon when a small lunch crowd filled up less than half the tables. The dinner crowd wasn't much bigger.

He headed back to the kitchen to get the bucket and mop. One waitress had already swept the dining room floor, and he agreed to handle the mopping. It was his first day in the diner working with Carole Ann and Amy. He liked it, altogether a different experience than his time with Jim.

For starters, they didn't treat him as the enemy, but as someone worth knowing. It would've been easy to make him feel like an interloper, the two of them worked well together. They didn't need another cook in the kitchen. He snorted at his own bad joke and turned out the lights on his way to the back.

Carole Ann ran the back of the house, the menus, the orders, the cook staff, dishwashers. Amy ran the front of the house, waitstaff, hostess, as well as managing all the books. They were a well-oiled machine, and it showed.

He pushed through the swinging door and surveyed the people he'd spent the day with. He liked each of them, even the teens took pride in the work they did.

"We ended up with a decent day," Amy yelled to no one in particular. She reconciled the day's receipts, a stack of money on the desk next to her. Carole Ann, her arms buried up to her elbows in rubber gloves, scrubbed away the grease on the gas stove with meticulous detail. Something his Kitchen Management teacher drilled into his students, *Grease fires are a menace in all restaurant kitchens* still burned forever in his head. The kid running the dishwasher started another load of glasses, and two of the waitresses chatted in the corner about the dismal night's tips.

The weighted warmth of peace settled into him, and he whistled a tune as he grabbed the mop and bucket. He stopped midway to the sink. *Where did he know the tune from?* It was familiar. Images flipped through his mind like a movie trailer. Plain interior, seat kicking, and loud childish singing laced with laughter. How could he forget the two boys from the plane trip here? He shook his head and laughed at himself. He scanned the room and hoped no one caught the slip. Humming childish Christmas tunes might ruin his reputation. The song still bounced around in his head as he filled the bucket.

He'd been working in restaurants most of his life. Part-time in high school and college. He was more at home in this environment than anywhere else. The pay was lousy unless you were a head chef. Unfortunately, gaining the experience didn't support his bills.

He slid the mop across the floor, working his way toward the office and Amy. "Mind if I mop in here?"

She nodded, but her attention never left the computer screen.

Not the invitation he hoped for, but it worked. He counted to fifteen before he asked his next question. "How long have you worked here?" He tried to sound casual while he continued working.

"Um... Quinn and I waited tables when we were in high school. She's been working here longer."

If she'd been working with the Wagners since she was a child, it was no wonder she took care of everything and everyone. They'd groomed her for it.

"How long has Quinn worked here?" He leaned on the mop handle and waited for her to answer, more anxious than he cared to admit for her reply.

"Since she first came to live with them, I guess. You could always find her shadowing one or the other." She stopped mid-count and gave him her full attention. "You know, now I think about it, in the beginning, she spent a lot of time with Emerson. He seemed to have a real soft spot for her." She wrapped a rubber band around the stack of bills and tucked it into the bank bag. "I forgot about that. I remember my mom saying something about what a joy it was to see how attached the two became." She stood up and grabbed the money bag, "I have to put this in the safe. I'll be back."

He finished up in the kitchen and worked his way to the dining room. Someone had already stacked the chairs on the table, making his job easier.

He'd finished the last pass when all the employees streamed out the back en mass as they chattered like blue jays about the party later that night. He locked the door behind them and flipped off more lights.

"Not so fast, we still have our weekly overview to get through." Carole Ann beamed as she came through the door with three cups of hot chocolate. Amy followed with a laptop and a large notepad. It touched him that they would include him.

The two women sat at the table, and Amy lit the candle. Ash flipped the chair around before he straddled it and reached for the hot chocolate. The last time he had hot chocolate, two winter storms had ripped through Texas, dropping over five inches of ice in Houston. He was twelve. He remembered it with clarity since that year he and Eric spent their first Christmas together with their grandparents. His father and Maria had only been married a few months, and she wanted to go away for their first holiday together.

"Is this your ritual?" He asked.

Carole Ann nodded. "It's a good time for Amy and me to compare notes, see what worked for the week, what didn't. Decide what specials are on tap for the week after next. Plan the orders."

Amy opened her laptop and typed. "Every Friday morning, we meet with Quinn and kind go through the combined plan. How long has it been since we did a meatloaf special?" She scrolled through the screens.

Ash tuned them out. He had no interest in the upcoming specials. In two weeks, none of it would matter if he got his way. Nothing would matter if the ski resort bought them out. His shoulders slumped, and a sour taste hit his mouth.

He needed to focus on the critical things. Whatever that was. He'd lost his edge, and he wasn't sure where the priority was anymore.

"Quinn set the cookie baking for this week, have you ordered everything for that?" Amy asked.

"What's the story with Quinn?" He blurted.

Both women stopped what they were doing and stared at him, the awkward silence between them growing to a monstrous size.

"I meant... I mean, I'm curious how she ended up here. That was wrong—"

"Well, none of us knows the full story," Amy spoke first. "From my perspective, she showed up one day in the middle of seventh grade. We had advisory, lunch, and another class together, and the Principal assigned me to show her the ropes. She was quiet, miserable, I didn't understand why. But she was nice, and I kept sitting with her, and before long, we became friends."

Amy paused, shaking her head as if trying to dislodge musty memories. She chewed the cuticle on her thumb before continuing. "It's a small town. There were all kinds of speculation and rumors. I think those hurt her more than anything."

"It did, and we should be ashamed of ourselves." Carole Ann scrubbed the handle of the mug, her jittery leg rattled the chair. "The Wagners volunteered no information either. Henrietta would tell me it was Quinn's story to tell if she ever wanted to tell it. I know she meant well, but I think it added fuel to the fire."

The candle flame flickered and danced to some unfelt breeze. It dared him to ask the one question he burned to ask. "No one knows what her issue with fire is?"

In unison, both women gasped in a breath and lowered their lashes, glancing away.

He'd crossed the line and had no business asking that kind of question.

Amy tipped over the chair in her haste to break the uncomfortable silence he'd created with the insensitive question. "Sorry." She set the chair right and asked if anyone else needed more cocoa.

"No, I'm sorry. I crossed the line. It's painful to watch her sit on the sidelines when it's obvious she wants to be a part of the activities." The Saturday S'mores party sprang to mind.

Everyone enjoyed the party, and it wasn't right. The person who planned it couldn't be in the mix of things.

Amy hurried to the back for more cocoa, leaving him alone with Carole Ann. "All any of us has is speculation. Neither she nor the Wagners ever shared the story of why or how she came to be here. All I know is her family died when she was thirteen. She had no other relatives. Emerson knew the family, friends with the grandmother or grandfather." She stopped to drain her cup.

It didn't take much to connect the dots in that story.

"She's never told anyone what happened? Not even Amy?"

Carole Ann shook her head. "Not that I know of. Her fear of any kind of fire is... a part of her. I don't think any of us question it anymore."

How had she managed to hide something this big? It made his chest tightened to think she'd buried the fear so deep without anyone to talk to. There were plenty of people she could have turned to but didn't.

Carole Ann broke through his thoughts. "Now, let me ask you a question." She pinned him with a stare. "What do you and your brother intend to do with your share?"

Ding-ding, the million-dollar question. He willed all emotion from his face, but his stomach rolled. The pulse beneath his ear throbbed. "I, we, the three of us, will discuss the best way to proceed at the end of this month." He ran a knuckle along his jawline. If the ski lodge had its way, lives would be forever changed, and Elf Hollow would lose its charm.

And he no longer wanted that. He didn't know what he wanted.

"The Wagners never had children. When Quinn came along, they seemed to feel as if their family was complete. Hope you boys can see the beauty and the benefit of all this."

She waved her hand to include the room. "Because Quinn is not going to let this place go without a fight. It's her home, and she's loyal to everything Henrietta and Emerson built. She came home to help take care of him when he took ill. Blood or not, they were her family, and that girl isn't going down without a fight."

That's what he was afraid of.

They finalized their plans for the upcoming weeks and walked out together. "Can I drive you to the B&B?" Carole Ann offered.

"Nah, it's a nice night. I think I'll walk." He waved his goodbyes and pulled his collar around his neck to head home. That thought nearly stopped him in his tracks. Home. And when did twenty degrees become a nice night?

He'd hoped to gain clarity after the night's conversations, but all it offered was more confusion. Quinn needed this town, and this town needed her. Carole Ann was right, she wouldn't sell, her loyalty and heart belonged in Elf Hollow.

Eric's voice nagged at him. Could he be that guy? The one that tricked someone into marriage to gain what he wanted? He pictured the way her smile warmed everyone who cared to notice. The way her musical laugh filled a room. The errant strand of hair she stubbornly tucked behind her ear a thousand times a day. Even the way she drank her coffee made him chuckle.

His heart pitched and stuttered, choking off his breath for a split second. He knew then he was gone. He either convinced her to sell because it's what she wanted, or he walked away with nothing.

In the past, the idea of waking to the same woman every morning suffocated him, sent him running for the door. But, for the first time, he could imagine a world where Quinn curled in his arms every night, and her smile greeted him every morning.

Chapter Fifteen

Niko dropped his tennis ball in her lap and stepped back. Tail thwacked back and forth as he gazed at her with eager anticipation. "Not now, Niko, I have too much work to do for playtime. Later." She tossed the ball on the floor and turned her attention to the mountain of paperwork that shouted for attention.

Eight a.m. Monday morning, and she was already behind. She had four days to complete the preparations for the yearly party they hosted for the North Shore Retirement Center, and they hadn't even started preparing. Hopefully, the diner had ordered the food. They still needed to set up the cookie decorating party for the kids, and she didn't even want to think about the bills.

She scrubbed a hand over her face, then nose-dived onto the desk. How did she let this happen? Her to-do list remained unfinished, and the things that got started ended up half done. Tossing her pen on the desk, she fell back into the chair.

Who was she kidding? She knew where to put the blame. At the feet of the tall, blonde male invading her home and her space.

She had no clue where the brothers stood and found her thoughts fixated on Ash way more than they should be. Would he sell? Would he persuade Eric to keep it and let her run things? Would he be the one to come back and check in if they kept it?

She straightened. Enough was enough, she cleared her head of all things Ash and picked up her pen. Time to get through the mess today. Even if she had to sit there until bedtime. No excuses.

"Does someone chain you to your desk every day?" The smooth rumble of her obsession's voice thundered in the quiet room.

Quinn's heart rate jumped from chill to jazzed in half a blink. Great. "Obviously not, or I wouldn't have this mountain of work as a reminder of how behind I am." She shuffled papers to hide the shaking of her hands.

"I don't know how you do it all. It's a wonder you don't stay behind." Ash moved into the room and took the seat across from her. His movements, smooth and confident, and his current expression chipped away at her resolve.

Faded jeans, cowboy boots, and a plaid shirt stretched taut over well-muscled biceps made her mouth water. With shoulders wide enough to block the world, it was all she could do to keep her focus on the conversation, much less the desk work.

She wished she could crawl inside that mind of his, dig around until she knew what to make of him. What did he plan to tell Eric about all this?

"What can I do for you?" She asked.

"Wondering when the snowmobile tour goes out. The brochure said the tour is today. I met John in town the other day, and Betsy said he is the best at tour rides."

"He is." She gave a minuscule nod of her head. Not what she expected. "But, we canceled the tour a few hours ago. No one signed up. I sent John home. Were you planning on taking the tour?"

He crossed his ankle onto his knee and leaned back, his hands entwined behind his head. "I was thinking about it, yes."

A fist around her lungs made it impossible to draw a deep breath. Did he know what he was doing to her, or did he do charming naturally?

He tapped the desk. "Quinn, did you hear me?"

She bit back a gasp. The same feeling a child gets when caught with their hands in the cookie jar rolled through her. "If you wanted to take the tour, you should have signed up." She didn't mean for it to come out so harsh. "I might be able to get John to take you out tomorrow."

"That won't work. I have phone meetings in the morning, and I work in the diner in the afternoon."

"Oh." She tapped her pen on the desk. As cold as it was outside, sweat trickled down the skin of her back.

"I have a brilliant idea. Why don't you take me?"

"Me?"

"You're the one that told me about the snowmobile ride to the waterfalls the first walk we took. You lit up like your Christmas tree out there when you talked about it. You should be the one to take me."

"I'm sorry, did you miss the desk plastered in paperwork?"

"No. But I think you need to take a break and show me around."

Her brain worked with a frenzy to come up with a plausible excuse to get out of doing this. She couldn't be alone with him. "Why don't I see if John can take you?" Maybe he hadn't left yet or was on his way back.

"I'm sure Henrietta would have wanted you, but I understand if you're too busy."

She ignored the hurt on his face and picked up the two

way. "John, you there?" She waited a few seconds and then tried again. Please, please pick up. "Yo, John, you there?"

"Sorry, I'm here. Helping the Samuels. They had a few trees down on their trails from the storm last week. What do you need?"

"How are our trails? Any problems?" Blocked trail equaled no ride.

"Nope, we're good. Few branches and twigs, nothing major, but I cleaned those off for the tour today."

Her heart stuttered. "Are you about done out there? I have a rider that would like to go out."

"Not really. We just started. I'm guessing it will be most of the afternoon. I guess I could come back if you need me to. I'll have to see if I can get someone else to help them."

She tugged at her earlobe, it would be so easy to tell him to come back, but she'd given him the afternoon off. Besides, the Samuels had been an enormous help when Emerson took ill and when Henrietta died. It wouldn't be right to leave them in the lurch. "Don't worry about it. Get them cleared up."

"Well, that's a real shame." Ash leaned forward and pinned her with his intense amber gaze.

He didn't appear all that broken up. Maybe it was the cocky grin and mischievous way his fingers rubbed at his temple.

He stood up and walked to her side of the desk. "Come on. I think you should take me. What are you afraid of?"

"No, no, no. I am not afraid. I've got way too much on my plate to go play."

Warm hands pulled her to her feet. "I won't take no for an answer. You look tense and stressed. This will be good for you." He scanned the papers. "Shouldn't I be learning about all this, anyway? I'll help you when we get back. Like I said, I'd bet Henri would like you to be the one to show me around. Don't you?"

Her stomach danced and fluttered. Who was she kidding? She wasn't strong enough to say no. "Okay fine. But be prepared. You *will* help me when we get back."

They took twenty minutes to find snowmobile pants in his size from the supply they kept for guests and, John had an extra pair of boots at the house Ash borrowed. They were small, but they would do. It was another thirty minutes before she finished his short lesson on the use and safety of snow-mobiling.

"Here." She handed him a black helmet and donned her own red one. "These have two-ways, we'll be able to talk."

Ash didn't move but stared at her with a look she couldn't read.

"What? Do I have something on my face?" She glanced in the hall mirror, but nothing appeared out of place.

"You're fine, but even wrapped up in all this snow gear, you're prettier than twelve acres of pregnant red hogs." The Texas drawl, that he turned on and off at will, skimmed across her skin like a butterfly's kiss.

His actual words sank in. *Huh?* Their gazes locked, and her jaw dropped. She sputtered, and laughter bubbled out of her. "What does that even mean?"

"I have no clue. I heard some guys use the line on one of my visits to the oilfield. It sounded fun, so I filed it away for future use."

"And this struck you as the right time?"

"What can I say? I have a knack."

"For what? Outrageous comments?"

"For making you laugh." His eyes burned with an amber glow that sent a shiver through her body.

She dropped the visor and turned away. "Let's get going."

Ten minutes into the ride and her stress levels dropped. The bitter bite of cold, the smell of snow and nature worked its magic as it always did. She loved the thrill, the live-action rush of excitement as she glided over the snowpack at high speeds. Adrenaline surged through her as she accelerated.

She'd planned to stay on the main trail, the one they used for all the guest tours, but at the last minute, she changed her mind. She had a pulsating desire to find out what Ash would think about one of her favorite spots.

"Take your speed down and be ready for a hard left," she said into the mic.

It was a longer ride and steeper climb, but when they reached the destination, she couldn't contain her anticipation.

Turning off the power, she removed her helmet and put it on the seat. "What did you think?"

"That was sweet." Ash followed her lead. "What a rush. We whizzed by some mighty big logs and trees."

"Sorry about that. I know I said it would be an easy ride, but I thought you'd want to see this place. Few tourists come here. They stay on the main trails."

Ash dropped a causal arm on her shoulder and gave her a squeeze. "I loved it. No need to apologize, darlin'. Where are we headed now?"

She pointed past the tree line. "Up that hill about a quarter-mile. Wait for it. You'll like this even more." She loved coming here, it was her favorite waterfall no matter the season, but this time of year, it was a winter oasis.

"You weren't kidding about being off the beaten path."

The hike took them another twenty feet up and over. As they reached their destination, she came to a stop and stood in awe of the surrounding majesty. No matter how many times she came to this spot, she never tired of the view. A work in progress. Ice formed and shifted, with the constant change in temperature and flow of water.

"I bet..." Ash came to a dead stop next to her, and whatever he planned to say died as he gazed out over the horizon. It was early enough in the season that portions of the falls cascaded over the rim in a roar while other sections already stood like ice-sculptures at a banquet. It never failed to work its magic on her.

"This is incredible. Where are we?"

"Welcome to Rainbow Falls." Her heart thundered with excitement as she led him to a pile of rocks and stones and took a seat. They settled into a groove close enough they shared space.

Silence blossomed around them. The solid warmth of his arm around her shoulder, the line of his body next to her. She imagined herself melting, pooling into a frozen puddle of hormones and exposed nerves.

"If money was no object, what would you do? Where would you go?" Ash asked.

His question caught her off guard. Definitely, not where her mind had been going. "Well, I never thought about it, but I guess ... here." She surveyed her surroundings. "I love it here. It's special. When I was away at college, I counted the days until I could come back. I can't imagine my life anywhere else. What about you?"

"I wish I could say I'd found my place, I haven't. But I know what I would *do*. I would open a restaurant. Probably in downtown Houston. Swanky and expensive."

"Oh. From what I tasted that first night, you should be very good at it. Why haven't you done it already?"

He studied the falls in silence. She'd all but given up on his answer when he cleared his throat. "I guess I kind of floated on the wave too long. You know what I mean? There's a certain path that is expected of you. And you fall into the rut. My father has never been my fan, but he's all about appearances. And in his mind, a chef would not have lived up to the great Joe Larsen's standards."

"Do you think owning the restaurant will make a difference to him?"

"I used to think that, but I don't really know anymore."

Disappointment made her breathing heavy. Silly, but there it was. Some part of her wished, more like hoped, he might stay. She reached for his gloved hand, wishing she could feel the heat of his skin against hers. Did selling his share of the inheritance make his dream happen?

He glanced at their joined hands. Unfamiliar emotions raced across his face. *What?* Desire, yes, but the other emotion? He was so close his breath warmed her cheek. His hand cupped her chin, and his thumb caressed her lower lip, the wool of his glove rough against the sensitive nerve endings. The word *run* echoed in her head. But she couldn't move even if she wanted to. And she didn't want to.

The sharp need for her kiss sent Ash over the edge, and his pulse quickened.

Her flushed complexion and parted lips, moist from licking them, were an invitation he wasn't strong enough to resist. What would she do if he kissed her? Would she pull away from him, or would she melt into his side?

The pink tip of her tongue slipped along the crease of her mouth. Pupils dilated, turning her iris almost black, and her breaths became shallow. "What are we doing?" She whispered, and squirmed and her body sank closer to his.

Ash groaned and lowered his head.

"Over here. I think it's just ahead." Someone shouted behind them.

They pulled apart with enough momentum, Ash fell out of the safety of the rock and slid sideways down the hill until he stopped at the feet of the hikers.

"Oh my gosh, are you okay?"

Not the happy ending he'd hoped for. He got to his feet

with the help of the newcomers and Quinn, who's body trembled with uncontrolled laughter.

"I'm fine. I might have fractured my ego, but I've been dinged worse." He chuckled.

Once he assured them he no longer needed their assistance, the hikers waved goodbye and left them alone.

Quinn looked like she wanted to bolt down a rabbit hole, the devious curl flicked at her cheek, and she reached up to brush it back. He doubted she even knew her fingers strayed to her parted lips as she continued to hold his gaze.

"I think." She licked her lips. "I think we should get back, it's getting late." She didn't wait to see if he followed but hustled down the trail to where they left the snowmobiles.

Tremors came to life in his gut, like a ball of bat wings coming awake at dusk, and a strange sensation clutched at his heart. He wasn't sure what happened, but one thing was certain, he would never be the same.

Chapter Sixteen

A sh turned on the light to his room and tossed his coat, hat, and gloves on the bench at the foot of the bed. Flipping the switch for the fireplace, he dropped into the nearby chair and let his head fall against the back. He stretched muscles knotted with so much tension they quivered with anticipation, and his body tingled like fire ants danced across his skin. The ride back from the falls did nothing to cool the heat coursing beneath the surface.

The memory of what almost happened on the trail looped in instant replay, giving him no rest. He jumped from the chair.

Cradled in the rock with Quinn in his arms, he'd been so close to the taste of sweetness. Lips lush, and ripe for his kiss... *One problem.* He didn't do sweetness. He liked his women, bold, brash, even a bit abrasive. None of which described the woman who currently took up residence in his brain.

He flexed his fingers and paced the room before he retook his seat.

Quinn ghosted the second they got back to the house, and

he didn't blame her. If those hikers hadn't come along when they did that kiss would have happened. He wanted it. She wanted it. He didn't misread the desire that darkened those eyes.

He ran a hand through his hair. Everything was muddled, and he was more confused than ever about what to do. Nothing would change Quinn's mind. She wasn't going anywhere, and selling his and Eric's half to the highest bidder would turn her life into one long nightmare.

Each day that passed, it got harder and harder to keep it all business. He checked his watch. Seven o'clock. His father had left a message for him while he was out with Quinn. Now was as good a time as any to call him back. Nothing like a talk with his dad to cool any lingering desire.

He took out the phone and examined it as if it held all the answers. His thumb worried the hard edge of the case. What did the old man want? He had the same jumble of emotions that plagued him most of his childhood whenever his dad would call him into the office. Those tingly nerves, sweaty palms, the bright-eyed, eager look of a child desperate for his only parent's approval.

After all these years, did he honestly believe his dad would call out the blue, with a change of heart? He punched in the speed dial and waited. His breath coming too fast.

"Took your own sweet time calling me back. Did I tear you away from something important?" Thick sarcasm oozed from his father's voice. So much for a change of heart.

"Ash? You there?"

Where else would he be? "Yea, I'm here."

"What's happening up there? Eric said that woman is giving us a hard time about selling. Have you seduced her to our side yet?"

"*Our* side?" He jabbed. "And who said anything about

seducing?" It must be killing the man that he didn't get a dime.

"It's the only thing you're good for, how else do you plan on getting to her?"

"Maybe your persuasive charm would work," Ash grunted.

"Can the smart-aleck routine and answer my question. Have you changed her mind?"

Ash's chest tightened. "No, dad, I haven't. It's not that easy."

"What good is all that swagger and crap of yours if you can't coax one woman to do what you want?" His father was the king of finding someone's weakness and using it to gain his way. Something Ash would never do.

Ash's nostrils flared, and his teeth ground until his jaw cracked. "It's not like that. *She's* not like that. There is an entire town here that relies on the businesses Henrietta and her husband built. Quinn is looking out for all of them. She's a better person than you or I will ever be."

"What the world needs. Another bleeding-heart idealist."

An unfamiliar protective instinct surged through him, and he launched from the chair. His blood pressure pounding at the crown of his head. His hand curled at his side. "You leave her out of this, you hear me, you bitter old man? She's filled with compassion, caring, and loyalty, things you'll never have. You have a problem with me go for it, I'm used to it, but don't you *ever* say a word against Quinn again." His breath came in ragged, shallow gasps, and black stars floated in his vision.

The silent pause dragged on for so long Ash wondered if he'd hung up, but the heavy breathing from the other end of the line told him otherwise. His father had never been speechless.

"It's property you never knew about, it's cash in your

pocket. Why do you care? I would think you of all people would want that since your grandmother was smart enough to lock up your trust fund. She knew what an irresponsible loser you are."

Ash gripped the phone until he thought it would break in half. That wasn't true, his grandmother loved him, but it didn't ease the sting of the words. "You know as well as I do, it's only until I get married."

"And we know that ain't happening. Losers like you end up alone."

Heat drained from his face. The room spun, and it was all he could do to keep the nausea at bay. "Better alone than bitter and angry."

Silence stretched too long.

"This isn't why I called." His father broke the silence.

"You mean there's more?" Ash took the time to bring his breathing back to normal and let the anger roll off him.

"I'm calling about the Jackson fiasco."

Ash wondered how long it would take his father to come at him about that. He'd almost forgotten about it.

"You have anything to say for yourself?"

"What's there to say? I think my actions were loud and clear." Not firing Alfred Jackson was a bold move that would guarantee his father's wrath, but he also refused to fire a man who'd been a loyal employee for more than fifteen years because of a life-threatening illness in his family.

"You blatantly ignored my orders to fire the man. In any other instance, that would be grounds for firing. I checked with our attorney, and there is nothing I can do to fix this. You've obligated us to pay him a year's salary and continue his insurance coverage, out of *our* pocket for a full year."

"That was the point." This conversation needed to end. There wasn't much more to talk about, and he had the sudden urge to be with people who liked him.

"You're too much like your mother. All soft and worried about the world." Labored breathing was the only sound as the seconds ticked by. "She was always fighting for a cause."

"I can't think of a better person to be like."

"You know, I'd fire your butt right now if your grandfather hadn't tied my hands, but his will ensured you would be protected. For now."

His grandfather's will? What did that have to do with anything? His head snapped to the side. A sinkhole opened in his gut, and a new wave of bitterness flooded through it. "What does Grandpa's will have to do with my job?"

"That's right, smart boy doesn't know about that. Seems my father felt you needed protection from me. His will stipulates I can't fire you. Unless you do something illegal or immoral, I'm stuck with you." The frost in those words carried more bite than the northern winds that blew through town.

Ash dropped onto the bed, his mind numb. All this time, he thought, *hoped,* his father kept him around because deep down, some part of him cared.

What a fool. His father would never love him. Grandpa kept him employed, and Gran tied up any means he would have of getting out from under the tyrant. He was beginning to wonder if anyone in his family cared about him. "Let me save you the hassle. I quit."

He took the phone from his ear, but his father's words reached him before he disconnected. "Don't mess this up for your brother." The words, spiked with disgust, dripped with disappointment. They might as well have been a knife stabbing him between the shoulder blades. He would never learn. The man would never forgive him the sin of being born no matter how hard he tried.

He tossed his phone on the bed. He wouldn't need it. He had no desire to talk to anyone who needed to call him. He turned off the fire and grabbed his coat. A brisk walk would clear his head.

Quinn entered the diner right before closing. She'd called earlier and told Carole Ann to hold her dinner but send Ash's to the house. Since they'd come back from their ride, she'd kept to herself, even grabbing her paperwork and escaping to the cottage. She wasn't ready to face him. Not yet.

"Quinn, over here," Amy called.

She hung up her coat and turned, a forced smile plastered to her face.

And froze.

The one person in the world she wanted to avoid sat with her friends as if he hadn't a care in the world.

She moved in slow motion, legs, stiff, wooden sticks. As she approached the table, the chair next to Ash slid out.

An invitation from the devil himself. With his booted foot still pressed against the leg and the raised eyebrows daring her to sit, it didn't take a genius to figure out who offered the chair.

"We had a deal," he said, his voice almost a deep purr.

She could think of nothing but the reckless-kiss-that-almost-was. "What?" She flinched at the breathless word.

"You take me on a ride, I help with paperwork. I tried to uphold my end of the bargain."

"Oh, that. I... um, it turns out there wasn't that much to do." She took a deep breath and turned to Carole Ann. "I thought you were going to send Ash's food up to him?" The words were forced from between her compressed lips.

"He came down before I could get someone to take it. Let me get yours." Carole Ann left for the kitchen and came back with a huge plate of spaghetti and meatballs.

All right, she could do this. Be natural. Laugh. Eat. Talk. Act like nothing *almost* happened.

Pretend she didn't wish it had.

Chapter Seventeen

"**P**ut this box over there for the kid's tree." Quinn handed Ash a stack of plastic Christmas ornaments for the kids. They'd spent the last thirty minutes toting boxes down from the attic.

Young and old alike loved tree decorating day. But Ash surprised Quinn by taking part. "I thought you hated everything Christmas?" She teased. "I didn't expect to see you this afternoon."

"Let's say I've developed a new appreciation for the season." He tugged a strand of her hair before he tucked it behind her ear. "I like the food." He grabbed a cookie off the table and took a bite. "And the company isn't bad, either."

He'd been doing that ever since they both ended up in the diner the night before. A wink here. A look that lingered, too long. Any chance to brush a hand across her skin. Soft and tentative. As if he wanted her to get used to his touch.

"Where do we start, and how does this work?" His gaze roamed the stack of ornaments. The red and white stocking he picked up and twirled held his attention.

"Haven't you ever decorated a tree before?" She joked, but the confusion on his face told her it was true.

"Christmas wasn't a big holiday in my house."

"Certainly, you had a tree. And stockings." Everyone had a Christmas tree. "Right?"

"Everything in my house was for show. My father paid someone to come decorate the perfect tree for his yearly business party. The stockings hung didn't have names and remained empty."

Quinn's phone vibrated in her pocket. The caller ID displayed Karen from the retirement home. "Hi, Karen, is everyone ready for the party on Friday?"

"That's why I'm calling. Our handyman quit today. Left us with a mess and no one to get Christmas lights up. Do you know anyone who would help?"

"I'm not sure. Let me ask around." Her gaze fell on Ash and an idea formed. What better way for him to see the other side of this business? The charitable side. "On second thought, Karen. I have the perfect person. He's Henrietta's nephew, and he's here learning everything he can about how we run things. I'll send him with a couple of helpers. They'll be there in the morning." She finished the call, excited with the plan.

"I guess you volunteered me for something?" That maddening, perfect, dimple appeared on the side of his mouth. Sheer masculine energy surrounded him.

"You'll love it." She assured him. "I'll fill you in later."

Seven kids piled through the doorway into the living room and made a beeline for the kid tree with Niko on their heels. Their excitement was contagious.

Quinn let go of a deep belly laugh.

"Darlin', you should do that more often." Ash walked over to join the kids. "Who wants to teach me some Christmas songs?"

"Me," all the kids shouted at once.

"Looks like another great event, Quinn," Sam McCray said as he and his wife came into the room, followed by the others. The adults milled around talking and getting their drinks. The kids ripped open the boxes and dug right into the decorating.

"Hey, Quinn, where do you want the empty boxes?" One of the guests called out.

"Over by the steps is fine. Thank you."

The bell rang, and Quinn excused herself. "Hello, Chica. The party is here," Amy said as she came through the door and shoved a tray full of appetizers into Quinn's hands. "Carole Ann sent these over. She said to tell you she'll be around later." She grabbed the coat of the man behind her and pulled him inside. "This is Zed. I met him in the bookstore this morning. Zed, this is my best friend, Quinn."

Tall, lanky Zed took off his coat, nodded a greeting, and wandered over to the drinks.

"Charming," Quinn said.

Amy dropped an arm over Quinn's shoulder. "He's the tall, silent type. He's passing through. Out of here by tonight." Amy found strays of all kinds, the four-legged and the two-legged, and took them under her wing.

Amy took the tray of food to the table. "How's it going with the sexy Texan? I felt a lot of tension between you two last night. Everything okay?"

Quinn rolled her eyes. "*Ash* is fine. And I still don't know what he and Eric will do." She smoothed the cuff of her sweater. "I need to tell you something. About yesterday."

"Dish it." Amy grinned from ear to ear and pulled Quinn to the side so no one would overhear their conversation.

Quinn told her about the ride to the falls. "He kept up. Then I took him over to the rock bench, and we sat there for a few minutes. And then..." Her cheeks burned, and she took a deep, steady breath.

"He kissed you? I knew it." Amy slapped her thigh and pumped the air. "I knew something was up between you two last night. Carole Ann said, no, but I felt it. Was he good?"

"No, shhh. Ash will hear you. We never actually kissed, some hikers came along. But we were close."

"Did you want to kiss him?" Amy pranced like a child and grabbed Quinn's hands. "You did, didn't you? And you still do, don't you?"

"Keep it down," Quinn snapped. "I'm not sure what I want, and until I figure it out, I don't need the house knowing my business."

"Fine. I'll keep it to myself on one condition. You tell me when it happens. 'Cause it's going to happen. Pinky swear it." She held out her pinky. Amy raised one eyebrow and tapped her foot. "Well?"

Quinn couldn't hold back a chuckle, but she wrapped her pinky around Amy's. "What are we? Thirteen again?"

"Whatever. Remember your promise. I'm gonna find Zed. And Quinn? Don't overthink this. For once, go with it." She sauntered off on the hunt for Zed.

"What do I do with this?" Ash came up behind her and dangled a glass pickle ornament.

"Don't hang that yet. It's the last ornament on the tree. You hide it somewhere in the branches."

"Okay. Why a pickle, and why hide it in a tree?" A playful grin creased his face.

"Do you know nothing of Christmas traditions?"

Ash took a bite of a sugar cookie and shook his head no.

"The Christmas pickle originated in Germany, at least that's the way the story goes. Tradition says it's the last ornament on the tree. After all the children are in bed, you tuck it in the branches. The first one to find it Christmas morning will have a blessed year and an extra special gift." She twirled the ornament, the light from the room catching the green. The first gift the Wagners gave her was this pickle.

"The Wagners started the tree party my first Christmas with them. They wanted to do something. Before the party, they gave me this and told me the story behind it. It was their way of giving me a blessing for the year. I think they hoped it would help me let go..." Her voice faded.

She never talked about that night. For fifteen years she'd kept them buried. They were hers alone. At first, it was fear. Fear that somehow her parents would disappear if she talked about what happened. Stupid. Irrational. Childish fear. At some point, it became easier to hold it inside. She rubbed her hand up and down her arm and lowered her lashes to hide the tears.

"Mr. Ash, will you please help us?" One of the young girls, Becca, tugged on his sleeve, her blue gaze full of innocence. She clutched the angel tree topper bought for the kid's tree.

"You okay?" The warmth from his hand branded the skin of her upper arm. Worry lined his forehead.

Before she could stop herself, she reached up and smoothed the furrow between his brows. A flood of heat zinged along the nerve endings the instant she brushed his skin. "I'm fine, but your audience awaits."

He hesitated, but then he gave her a tentative smile and scooped Becca into his arms and spun around. "Let's go put that angel on the tree. Does it go on the bottom?"

The childish laughter floated back to Quinn as he walked away. Maybe the cocky mask he always wore slipped. Whatever it was, the man holding Becca up to place the angel on the tree to the cheers of seven children, was not the same one that came through her door two and a half weeks ago.

"He seems like a nice young man." Helen McCray moved into the spot Ash vacated and picked up an ornament from the box at Quinn's feet.

"The kids certainly like him."

"You know, Quinn, Sam, and I were sorry to hear about Henrietta." Her pale blue eyes, surrounded by age and life, held Quinn's gaze. "We've been coming here since we were first married and, with the exception of a handful of years, we've come back every Christmas. Why I think I've known Henrietta as long as any of my dear friends."

"I know Henri counted you among her close friends, Mrs. McCray."

The older woman laughed and patted her arm. "Call me, Helen, dear. It seems you are the lady of the house now. It doesn't seem possible." She pursed her lips and reached down for another decoration. "I can still remember the mite you were that first year. Sad and off in the corner all alone. It broke Emerson's heart to see you like that."

"They always hated when I hid in the corner."

"They did. But Emerson always worried you were unhappy. It was imperative to him you didn't feel alone. That you knew you had family and friends."

Quinn's throat closed. He was always kind to her. Doted on her. It took her a long time to accept him. Through the ignorance of childhood, she never realized how much he'd worried about her. She felt terrible for any sadness she caused him.

"Did you know Sam and I would never have met if not for Henrietta and Emerson?"

"I never knew that. What did they do?" First Jim Lovette and Ally and now Helen and Sam? What else did they hide from her?

Helen's expression softened as she seemed to lose herself in the memory. "Henrietta and I go way back. To our school days, in fact. She was two grades ahead of me, but we lived on the same street. I was overjoyed when she met Emerson, and they made the decision to move here and start the bed and breakfast. It was about a year after they opened, she called and offered me a free stay, but it had to be a particular weekend. I just had to agree to take word back home about the place."

"Let me guess. Sam was here that weekend."

Helen beamed. "He was, and the rest is history as they say. And we weren't the only ones."

That was a surprise. "There were more?"

"At least three other couples I know of. The Wagners had a knack for matchmaking. I think it was a hobby for them."

Quinn hung the ornament she'd been holding on a low branch, her thoughts reeling. She'd been blind when it came to her benefactors.

"I think you were next on the list," Helen said with a grin.

"Me? What makes you think that?"

"Henrietta worried about you. She didn't want you to end up alone."

Quinn thought about all the conversations she and Henri had since she came home from college. Now that she thought about it, Henri did ask a lot of questions about boys from the school. "Why?"

Helen waved an elegant hand in the air. "She feared you'd get wrapped up with this place and forget about love until one day, you would look up and realize it was too late."

Quinn fumbled and almost dropped the nutcracker in her hand. Henri worried about her all the time, but she hadn't realized how much until now. It's the reason she never told her about Ty cheating. Emerson and Henri were not fans of his. The one and only time they'd met him, at parent's weekend, it had been an instant and mutual dislike. She knew how angry Henri would be if she knew the full story.

But, that didn't mean she didn't want to find someone and settle down. She did. Someday.

"She would be thrilled to see you and your fella together."

"My fella?" Confusion wrinkled her nose.

Helen nodded toward Ash. "Henrietta would approve of that young man, I think."

"Oh, Helen, no. Ash and I aren't dating. He's—"

"You might not be now, but you will be. I can sense these things. And I have no doubt he is smitten with you."

Smitten with me? She peeked around the tree. Was it possible?

"It's too bad Henri didn't get to meet Ash in person. She spoke highly of him."

Wait, hold up. "She talked to you about him?"

"Well, yes. Sadie told her he struggled with his father and was a bit of a wanderer, but such a good boy. The last I talked to her, she said something about finding a solution to his problem."

Helen excused herself and joined her husband on the couch.

Quinn dropped into the nearest chair, far from the fireplace, but close enough to the window to glimpse the snowdrifts.

She searched out Ash and found him by the food table talking to Amy. A gorgeous example of a man. All fluid lines and supple muscle. The stubble of five o'clock shadow skimmed along his jawline, and when he laughed, something inside her answered, and lightness filled the space in her chest.

As if he felt her gaze, he glanced in her direction. A boyish grin on his face.

She didn't like where her thoughts headed. Was it possible? Could Sadie and Henri somehow planned for her and Ash to meet?

She peered out the window, big fat flakes drifted at leisure from the sky. Ridiculous. They couldn't pull something like that off.

Could they?

Chapter Eighteen

Ash dropped John at the house for a scheduled snowmobile tour after their morning at the retirement home. They'd strung the lights, finished the decorating, and even managed some handyman work that'd been long overdue.

The residents were ready for their party on Friday. A lightness filled Ash as they left. Satisfaction. It was an unfamiliar emotion for him. Working with his hands, being productive and appreciated was a new experience. And it didn't hurt several of the residents gave them four different tins of home-baked treats.

He walked to the diner for a late lunch before heading to the shop to work with Jim. At the tree decorating party yesterday, they'd formed a tentative truce, and Ash agreed to come down after his stint at the retirement home.

Other than a quick coffee at breakfast, he hadn't seen Quinn. He hoped she was all right. She'd almost shared something important from her past the night before. But then she allowed her concern for him to overshadow the memory.

He braced himself for the gust to slap him in the face as he rounded the corner, but for once, no wind. Or maybe he didn't mind the cold as much as he did when he first arrived.

With visions of hot coffee and a quick bite before his shift at the store, he picked up his speed the last few steps to the diner. Chaos greeted him as he opened the door. Music blasting from the speakers couldn't drown out the raised voices of angry customers. Two frazzled waitresses hustled from table to table.

He overheard one explain they were behind in the kitchen and offered an appetizer for their inconvenience. A quick scan of the dining room showed more annoyed faces and diners at a four-top about to leave.

Since when did Carole Ann get behind in the kitchen? From what he'd witnessed, she was too efficient.

Ash shrugged out of his coat and crossed the floor to the register. The young woman behind the counter stood like a statue, a flushed expression pasted on her face. "Sara, right?" He waited for her nod. "Where's Amy? I've never seen it like this. What's going on?"

"This is Amy's day off, but Quinn's in the kitchen."

Why would Quinn be in the kitchen? He pushed through the door to a kitchen filling with smoke. "What—?" He jogged around the divider to the cook station. Flames made their way across the griddle, from the grill section, toward the eggs, sausage, blackened bacon, and hash browns about to catch fire.

Quinn stood, frozen, spatula in hand. Complexion white, expression blank, her lashes fluttering too fast. The only other person nearby was a young dishwasher in the back with his headphones on, dancing to a beat only he could hear.

Ash stepped in front of Quinn and turned off all the burners, then grabbed the bucket of baking soda by the stove and threw it over the flames. Once the blaze was out, he turned and wrapped Quinn in his arms. With gentle tugs, he lured her away from the stove.

Tremors racked her body, and her teeth chattered. "It's okay, it's okay. It's out. Come here." He shuffled her away from the scene and rubbed his hand up and down her arms.

She shook violently against him. He picked her up and carried her to the office, where he kicked out the chair and sat with her snug in his lap. "It's over, no one's hurt, darlin'. It's okay."

"No. It's not okay, someone could have died." Her voice croaked, and she shook her head over and over. "I had no business doing this."

A small chuckle escaped before he could stop it. He didn't want to make light of Quinn's fear, but he wanted his confidence to rub off on her. What he tried to hide was the fear that slammed him in the gut when he saw the surrounding flames. "It was a small grease fire. Carole Ann keeps a spotless environment. No one was in danger. It would have burned itself out. You need to breathe. You hurt?"

Her arms tangled around his neck in a death grip. "That doesn't make me feel better," she mumbled into his shirt collar.

Okay, it was worse than he thought. No way she'd sprawl all over him otherwise. He nudged her out enough to do a quick search for burns. "Slow your breathing, honey, or you'll give yourself a heart attack. Slow, deep breaths." He breathed in and out until her breathing matched his. "That's a girl. You got this. Nice and slow."

"I'm... I'm fine. Not hurt." She took a huge breath and then another and then another. The quaking slowed. Tears clung to her lash line, threatening to tumble down her cheeks.

They sat there in silence while her heart rate came back to normal. He liked the weight of her in his arms, her hands cupped around his neck. A warmth pooled in the center of his chest where powerful need roared to life in him. The urge to protect her, made his arms tighten, and he pull her closer. "What happened? Where is Carole Ann?" At least the chaos that greeted him when he got here made sense.

Amy burst through the door. "What's going on?" She coughed and waved her hand. "Sara called and said the diner was on fire. What happened?" She charged into the office, along with all the other employees. "Where is Carole Ann?"

"Her husband called this morning, she slipped on ice on the way to the car. He had to take her to the emergency room." Quinn's lips brushed the pulse at his neck as she spoke.

"Why didn't you call me? Or Simon?" Amy asked.

Quinn sat up, calmer, voice almost normal. "I didn't want to bother you on your day off."

"Didn't want to bother... it's my job. I manage the diner, remember?"

Quinn flinched at the words. "I called Simon. He's on his way, but it was his afternoon off. I thought I could handle it until he got here."

"Hey, Amy, cool it. She doesn't need this right now." His newfound protective instincts flared to life.

"It's okay, Ash. She's right, I shouldn't have been back here. I thought I could do it."

"I'm sorry, Quinn. You know I don't want you hurt." Amy moved in to hug her friend. "Sara said you did fine until the fire."

A weak smile creased Quinn's face. "That's kind of her."

"It's okay. Nothing but a small grease fire. Never even left the grill top," Ash offered.

"And I'm fine. I'm not sure what happened. One minute I was trying to get the bacon off the grill, and the next, a flame shot up from the grill side. I must have spattered grease... I don't know. I froze. I couldn't move." An aftershock rocked through her.

"I'll go check the damage," Amy said.

"I don't mean to be crass, but should we close?" The cashier waited, lips pursed. "I have a lot of angry people out there?"

Someone wanted *him* to solve the problem.

Amy came back in with a look of relief on her face. "You're right, it's not that bad. Didn't even mark the wall behind the stove. We need to get the mess cleaned up, and we're back in business. How long ago did you call Simon?"

"He should be here anytime. He was scheduled for tonight. He was out when I got a hold of him." Quinn mumbled.

They had a restaurant full of people who'd waited a long time for their food. He could scour off part of the grill and be cooking within fifteen minutes. "No need. I'll cook. I'll have to get the grill cleaned off first. Do we have anything we can give to the customers willing to wait?"

"You can cook?" Amy was skeptical.

"Why does everyone always ask me that?"

"He's a great cook." Quinn attempted to lighten the mood and gave him a punch on the shoulder. "Makes a killer grilled cheese sandwich."

He lifted her chin. "You going to be okay? Do you need me to take you back to the house?"

She shook her head. "I'm going to sit here for a while. You go ahead. I'm feeling better already."

The confidence in her voice didn't hide the lie in her eyes, but he let it go. He stood and settled her into the chair.

Amy hustled out of the office and came back in a hurry with a glass. "Here. Drink this and take these." She handed Quinn two aspirin.

She swallowed half the water and leaned back.

Ash motioned Amy out of the office and left the door ajar.

"Offer anyone left out there a free appetizer to tide them

over. Tell them if they wait, their meals will be out in a few minutes and on the house. Barney," he called to the busboy, "get that scraper and help me scrape off the food and baking soda." He tied an apron around his waist and got to work.

"Ash, I'll go handle the front. Let me know if you need anything back here."

"Do me a favor, call Jim, and fill him in. He's expecting me later today."

Amy nodded.

They got through the lunch mess, and in between the stragglers, they got the kitchen back in shape. He didn't realize how much he'd missed being in the kitchen. It had been ten years since culinary school. He started working for Cayman Oil after college. By the time he realized how miserable he was, it was too late. He had bills and bills and more bills.

Guess that wouldn't be a problem anymore. Now he was jobless. Any paycheck would be a help. As much as he hated working under his father's thumb, the job had paid the bills.

Over the next couple of hours, everything he'd learned in school came back to him.

He went to the office. Quinn must have snuck out. He needed to pull up the email before he could go find her.

Carole Ann's husband called to tell them she'd broken her leg in three places and would be out of commission for the rest of the month. He emailed instructions she'd given him to pass on.

"Ash, Amy wants to know if you'll take over the kitchen while Carole Ann is out or if she should make other plans," Sara said, coming through the door.

He stopped what he was doing. Take over the kitchen? A chuckle rumbled in his chest. When he dreamed of his own place, he hadn't pictured a greasy spoon in the middle of *Wintertown*. He scanned the space, all clean and busy. "Tell Amy no need to find anyone else. I got it." He sat back in the chair and laced his fingers behind his head. This would do for now.

A fog still surrounded what happened with Quinn. Why she froze the way she did. But he was darn sure gonna find out. Lots of people had a fear of fire, but most didn't freeze at a simple grease flame.

He had his suspicions, but she needed to talk about it, or her fear would hold her hostage for life.

Like it or not, it was time for her to unload that baggage.

Chapter Nineteen

For an hour, Quinn paced the floor of her cottage, desperate for the peace the walls provided. Her cottage, her haven, her cave, whatever she called it, this was the place she came to lick wounds, and decompress. But today, the comfort of home eluded her. She wanted to crawl deep into a hole and pull the earth back. Anything to cover her humiliation. *God, how stupid could she be?* She had no business going into that kitchen.

Her hands shook with enough force to rattle the bones loose. Not wanting to see the evidence of her cowardliness, she shoved them under her armpits.

No matter how many times she replayed the scene, she couldn't see what happened. One minute she worked over the grill, something she'd never done before. Maybe she'd gotten cocky or too sure of herself, but the next, a flame shot straight up, the scorching heat a lick beneath her chin.

Then Ash held her and told her it was over. No memory of anything between the two incidents. Raw terror. The kind that clawed like an alien exploding from your chest. That's all she could remember. What would have happened if Ash hadn't gotten there when he did? The only one around had been the dishwasher lost in the music blasting through his earbuds.

Ash tried to laugh it off, a minor grease fire, nothing dangerous. But then, few people understood the life-force of a fire. The beast that haunted her nightmares for the last fifteen years attacked. And she'd lost.

Again.

Someone knocked on her door. "Quinn, you in there?"

She stumbled around the corner from the kitchen and scraped her knee on the corner of the coffee table. Tears stung as they rolled down her cheeks. "Ouch," she whispered.

"Quinn? You okay in there?"

What was he? A superhero with x-ray hearing? Or was that x-ray vision? She shook her head and pushed the mindless babble to the back of her mind.

Another knock. "Quinn? I know you're in there."

She froze. Her spine stiffened, and a knot the size of the giant pineapple on her kitchen counter agitated her stomach. What was he doing there? For a second she contemplated climbing out the bedroom window, but she needed her boots and coat which hung by the door. The door Ash stood on the other side of.

She needed to be quiet, and he'd go away.

"If you don't answer the door, I'm gonna have to find another way in, darlin'. I need to be sure you're not hurt."

"Fine." She spat the word between gritted teeth. The cords in her neck flexed in frustration. Why wouldn't he leave her alone? She needed to nurse her wounded ego. Was that too much to ask?

She hobbled across the floor to the tiled area that served as the entryway. The deadbolt clicked as it slid back, she didn't bother to open it.

He came in. Tall and handsome with that infuriating

dimpled grin that made her insides turn to mush. Arms strong enough to carry the burdens of life. But instead of mocking her for her weakness, he crooned his concern. Lulled her with soft murmurs and caress of his fingers as they brushed over the trail of tears.

Turning her back, she stalked to the couch where she dropped and curled into a ball. She didn't deserve concern. She deserved to wallow in self-pity and a gallon of mint chocolate chip ice cream. Which she didn't have. "Why are you here?" She mumbled into the pillow.

"I wanted to check on you."

"You did. I'm fine. You can go." She didn't know which made her crazier. The Ash that didn't care about anything, or the one that cared enough to trudge down here in the cold to check on her humiliation.

"You need fresh air. It's warmed up out there. Or at least that's what everyone keeps telling me. And I see people walking around with coats unzipped and no gloves. No clue how anyone would mistake thirty as warm. Personally, I think y'all are two sandwiches short of a picnic."

His quirky, Texan charm. Meant to make her laugh.

Anger propelled her to a sitting position, locked and loaded with a snarky reply.

But he stood there with a stupid grin on his face. Her boots at the ready, holding her coat.

And like that, her anger morphed into resignation.

"You're not going to leave me alone, are you?"

He shook the coat and smiled.

"Fine. But I'm not talking."

"A walk. Nothing else."

He led her out the door and headed toward the lake for the sunset. No wind, no snow, and temperatures a smidge above freezing. He'd been right, a gorgeous evening to be out.

"No gloating allowed, but you were right. It's a beautiful night."

"Shh. No talking." He tucked her hand under his arm. They strolled as if they were a couple in love with no worries between them. When they reached a bench, he waved, inviting her to sit, but he still kept his promise not to speak.

The Sawtooth Mountains rose from the horizon, encircling portions of the shore. For as far as the eye could see, the frozen lake reflected the hues of pink and lavender with glimpses of blue from the sunset behind them. Breathtaking as always. Her heart swelled. The peace that shunned her back at the cottage settled around her like a hug. Warmed her from the inside.

She stole a sideways peek at Ash. His strong profile, silhouetted against the sun's last flare of light, made breathing hard. How had he become such a part of her life in such a short amount of time? She remembered life before him, but the memory seemed two dimensional. Flat.

Who better to share with than a man who would be gone in a few weeks taking her sad, pitiful memories with him?

"One night, when I was thirteen — " She sank into her coat. She didn't want to do this. The need to run hammered at her. But for fifteen years, she'd tried to escape, and it had gotten her nowhere.

She took a deep, stuttering breath and tried again. "My mom and I fought. Don't even remember what it was about. Probably something angsty and childish. She sent me to bed early for being rude. I woke up around midnight, and everyone was asleep. I snuck down to the basement to watch the show I'd recorded earlier in the day. I must have fallen asleep because I woke up coughing with smoke filling the room. I tried to get upstairs to wake my parents, but when I reached the top of the steps, flames had already eaten through part of the floor. They were trapped." The memory of the blistering heat as it poured through the doorway, made her skin sizzle.

Ash grabbed her hands and warmed them by rubbing them between his own. The intensity of his gaze brushed her cheek, but she stared at his right earlobe. If she so much as glanced at him, she would dissolve into mist and float forever in the fog over the lake ...

"I ran back down and left through the basement door. I kept hoping I would find my family outside looking for me." A sob choked out the last word as she swiped at the tears that rolled down her nose. "But, they weren't."

She lunged from the bench and stumbled to the edge of the lake. Arms wrapped around her middle, desperate to keep herself from being blown apart by the sheer power of the emotion. The pain doubled her over as the tears flowed unchecked. How could she live with this pain? No wonder she'd kept it locked away for years. She needed to shove it back in the black hole and bury it deep enough it could never threaten her again.

The heat of his body engulfed her before his arms did. Instead of pulling away, she allowed herself to melt into him. To savor the comfort. The courage he gave her.

"By the time the firemen and police arrived, the whole house was engulfed in flames. My parents ... they died of smoke inhalation." The fact they never felt the flames always gave her some peace. "I should have tried harder to get them out."

She wasn't sure how long they stood there, but by the time the bone-jarring sobs stilled, it was dark, and the wind had picked up.

Ash tilted her head to face him. "You were a child, Quinn. There was nothing more you could do. Did you hear the smoke detectors?"

"No. I've spent too many nights trying to remember, but I

can't hear them. I know my mom used to nag my father about fixing them. I guess he never did." She swiped at her face with her gloved hand.

Ash grabbed her shoulders and gave her a shake, his stare holding her gaze. "You can't go on like this. The past won't give up its stories, but they belong in the past. You deserve happiness." He rubbed his thumb along her chin. "You deserve a life."

How many times had she tried to convince herself she didn't get to enjoy life? She lived and breathed while her family laid in the cold ground. Her brother was denied the chance at a life while she still walked. What right did she have to be happy?

"I don't think I can, Ash." She dropped her head on his chest and inhaled the warm cinnamon scent that always surrounded him.

He tipped her chin until she had no choice but to look at him. His lips caressed a tear that rolled from the side of her right eye, then the left. "You are beautiful." He followed the trail of tears down her cheek, "You're filled with kindness," to her jaw, "you are worthy." His lips nuzzled the corner of her mouth. "You have brightened my days and given me something no one else has." His mouth crushed hers in a red-hot kiss that chased the darkness away and ignited a light of hope deep within her.

Her mind screamed at her to step away, but the pulse pounding through her veins was a tidal wave that drowned out logic.

His arms tightened around her and pressed their bodies close enough a groan rumbled between them.

Being held, to be somebody's someone made her not want to think or reason. She wanted only to lose herself in the moment as it wiped her mind clean.

He broke the kiss and nipped her lower lip, a slow, sweet

smile brightening his face. "Come on. Let's go back to your place. If I stand here too much longer, I'll turn into a Popsicle."

Back at the cottage, he wrapped her in a blanket and nestled her into the couch. "Let me see if I can find something edible in that barren kitchen of yours."

He came back a few minutes later with a plate of pineapple, cheese, crackers, cold meat, and a bottle of wine with two glasses. "You don't believe in real, sink-your-teeth-into-it food. Do you?"

"You saw what happens when I cook. In case you haven't noticed, we have gas stoves everywhere. I suppose the fear I've carried all these years kept me from learning to cook. Everything can be nuked these days." The heaviness that crushed her chest twenty-four-seven eased.

"How did you end up here?" Ash asked as he cut a hunk of cheese.

She shook her head. "No idea. They put me in a foster home for a few days, and then my social worker showed up to say she was taking me to my new home. That's all I know."

"There must be a reason you're here."

"No one ever told me. I heard something about Emerson being friends with my grandparents or something. I guess they didn't want to see me go into the foster system."

Later, as they cleaned up from the food, Ash found the box of letters the attorney gave them, sitting on the kitchen counter. He picked one up and scanned it. "It's strange to see my grandmother's handwriting. Have you read any more of them?"

"One or two a night. Take a handful with you. I think you'll enjoy them."

He took a few letters to read later and shrugged into his

coat. She stood still before him, hands tucked into her back pockets, and surveyed him. Petite. Fragile. Thumb print-sized smudges of blue, rimmed the hollows beneath her eyes. Her caramel hair flipped over her shoulder.

A lump formed in his throat. There was no two ways about it. Their shared kiss shattered everything he knew about kisses and it branded him.

"Ash, thank you. For today. Tonight. I... I—"

"You trusted me with something you've never shared with anyone else." He flipped a strand of hair when what he really wanted to do was steal another kiss. "Don't think I take that trust for granted. Good night, Quinn."

"Good night, Ash."

He stepped into the night air and listened for the click of her lock before he started to the main house. No one ever trusted him with something so personal. Then again, he allowed no one to get close enough to share.

By the time he got to the house, everyone had gone to bed. He heated a mug of hot chocolate and headed to his room. With its barrage of Christmas decorations and the multi-hued tree in the living room, it could pass as an advertisement for a home magazine. He jogged up the steps, a whistle on his lips.

Once in bed, he picked up the first letter and read through it. It still rocked his world that his grandmother was *the other* woman. It was hard to imagine his grandparents so young, making bad decisions. Being human.

He guzzled the last of the cocoa and scanned another letter. He got halfway through and stopped.

How is Quinn adjusting? Is she still waking with nightmares? His grandmother asked.

Ash flipped the envelope and noted the dated postmark right around the time Quinn came to live with Henrietta and Emerson.

That poor girl. I can't imagine what she's going through. I still

don't agree with Emerson's decision not to tell her the truth.

She deserves to know. I understand Emerson needs time to adjust to the

information himself, it must have been quite the shock. To both of you.

And it's none of my business, and I have no right to say anything, but

you know me, I can't ever keep my mouth shut.

All true. Even when she knew it would annoy someone, she always spoke her mind. But now the question was the cryptic message. What did it all mean? He searched the rest of the letters. Stories of him, his father, Eric. Curiosity about Henrietta's businesses. But nothing more about Quinn.

What if Quinn had read that letter? Were there others? The sisters may never have physically come together again, but it appeared they'd shared everything.

What other secrets were in them?

He turned off the light and tucked his hands behind his head. He made a mental note to call Cayman Oil's in-house inspector in the morning and ask him to do a search.

This mystery begged to be solved.

Chapter Twenty

Ash walked into the Christmas Shoppe, disappointed to find no customers. The Friday before Christmas, the place should be hopping. Where were all the last-minute shoppers? "Mornin' Betsy, where is everyone?"

"I have been asking myself the same question. I've only had two customers all morning." Betsy tapped her short, neatly trimmed fingers on the counter, her gray head bobbing.

"Jim in his office?"

The older woman, who ran the store on Fridays, grinned and waved him to the back. "He's waiting for you."

"Any idea what he wants? He doesn't normally work Fridays, does he?" He hadn't talked with Jim since the tree decorating when they'd formed a tentative truce.

"Nope, but I don't think he's here to work."

Ash sauntered through the door to the back and walked the few steps to the office. Jim sat behind his desk, forehead wrinkled in concentration over something on his computer. Jeans, plaid shirt, winter vest, and a knit hat still on his head. Not his usual work attire.

"That frown doesn't look good," Ash said.

Jim waved him to the chair. "Our sales are a bit light for the month. Nothing to worry about." He shut down the computer. "Thanks for coming."

"Yea, sure. Did you want to talk about sales?" He wasn't sure how much help he would be, retail wasn't one of his strengths, but he'd give it a shot.

Jim shook his head. "That will fix itself. I thought we could get better acquainted."

"And how are you going to do that?"

Jim gave him a weak smile. "Ice fishing." He grabbed two short poles Ash hadn't noticed and led the way out the door.

"You and I are going ice fishing?" He cocked his head to the side. You could knock him over with a feather. What was the guy up to? His skin constricted with uneasiness. Why would the man want to take him fishing? They'd formed a tentative truce, not a friendship. "Tonight is the retirement home party, and with Carole Ann out, there's still a lot of prep work."

"Don't worry, I had Amy call in an extra cook to help. They've got it covered. We'll be back before they miss you."

"But I really think—"

"You're not indispensable," he snapped. "We got by fine before you came. I'm sure they'll manage this morning." He turned his head away before Ash could get a read on him.

"You can reach me on my phone if you need me, Betsy," Jim shouted as they walked out the door.

"You two have fun," she answered.

Ash's radar clanged, and his defenses went up as he followed the older man outside.

"This is me right here." Jim opened the door of an older model Jeep Wrangler.

They pulled into a public parking lot and headed to the dock where a couple of snowmobiles waited for them.

"Ever ridden?" Jim asked.

"Yea, twice. Quinn taught me."

"Of course, she did."

Ash wasn't sure how to take that comment. The man's body language and occasional snarky comments didn't match with the chummy attitude he projected.

"We're riding out to those two red buildings. It's still early in the season. By the end of January, it will be a fishing village on ice. Too bad you won't be around to see it. It's a sight, I tell ya."

It only took a few minutes to ride out to the cluster of brightly colored ice houses. The ride quickened his heartbeat as much as the ride with Quinn. He would miss this in Houston.

They parked, and Ash surveyed the area. The two metallic red buildings, belonging to Fisherman's Cottage, were a modest size and inviting like two miniature houses smack dab in the middle of the lake.

Jim pushed through the door, and they stepped into a warm, cozy environment.

"Wow, not what I expected from an ice house." Ash let loose with a long whistle of appreciation.

Jim chuckled. "What did you expect?"

Whatever he expected, it wasn't this. "I don't know. A wooden shack with no heat and men huddled around a black hole in the ice." Instead, he found a wood stove, kitchen, table, and a sound system with TV. Five comfy chairs each sat in front of a round covers in the floor, presumably the ice holes.

Jim slipped out of his coat and tossed his gloves on the table. He blew on his hands and rubbed them together. "It's cold today. I had John come by earlier to get the fire started. Take the chill off." He put two more logs inside. "Pick a spot and let's fish."

Jim handed him a pole.

Ash pulled a chair up to one of the covers and lifted the

lid. A blast of cold air hit him in the face. He stared into the abyss. Now what? He examined the hook at the end of the line and puckered his lips. Pretty sure something needed to go on there.

"Oh, yeah, check in that toolbox next to you. You'll find all the bait you want."

Ash slid the box closer and opened it to a fully stocked supply of bait, all organized in separate compartments. "Any particular one you recommend?"

"Don't matter. They all work. I usually bring live bait, but this was last minute. We'll have to make do with this."

Except for the occasional suggestion on how to hold the pole or bait for success, they fished in silence. The whole thing was bizarre. What were they doing out here? The prickle of unease he'd experienced back at the store returned, the tension settled like a weight between his shoulder blades.

Ash couldn't take it anymore. "So, what? Are we like best friends now? One call for a truce, and we're chill, ready to braid each other's hair and do our nails?" He glanced at the top of Jim's bald head. "Correction, you can braid my hair."

"You're a smart mouth, aren't you?" Jim's face turned red with anger.

"That's the first real thing you've said all morning."

"You got an answer for everything."

"That's where you'd be wrong. I don't know a darn thing. Including why we're here playing this game." He scrubbed his free hand over his face. And the longer he stayed in this town, the less he understood. "Why don't you cut to the chase and tell me why you brought me here."

Jim declined to answer. He sat and stared into the black hole.

Ash's stomach knotted. He couldn't help himself. If there were a way to sabotage a good thing, he would find it.

"I tried to make this casual. It could've been about fishing," Jim said.

"I'm sorry. I'm not used to people offering an olive branch."

"No, you were right. I brought you out here to find out what your plans are. You and your brother."

Ash jangled his fishing line, stalling for time. He didn't have a good answer. Not anymore. "Ask me that three weeks ago I'd had an answer for you. We even had the potential buyers set up. But it's not that easy anymore. It gets complicated once the players become real."

"Sounds like you might be having a crisis of conscience," Jim said

Understatement of the century. Either he disappointed his father and brother, or he disappointed Quinn and the town. No matter how he sliced it, he couldn't see his way clear of the dilemma. "Guess so."

"Whenever I find myself in a corner, I talk to people I trust. What does your father or mother say about all this?" Jim pulled his pole out of the water and changed out the bait.

"My mother died a long time ago. And trust me, my father is not a man I would turn to for trusted and valued advice. He'd as soon sell-off this entire town as look at any of you." Who did he turn to? His grandmother used to be his sounding board.

"Way I see it, your aunt brought you here for a reason. She must have felt you would do the right thing."

"My aunt didn't even know me. She had no clue what I'd do." He thought of the letters back in his room. His grandmother didn't pull her punches, she might have shared everything with Henrietta.

"I worked for Henrietta a long time. The woman never met a stranger. And she saw redeeming qualities in everyone. Neither she nor Emerson encountered a stray they didn't think they could help." Jim dangled his line, and he shook his head. "I don't think you are here by luck of the draw."

Ash pondered the statement. "The land alone is more valuable than any monthly income we could collect. What would you do? Would you walk away from it all for a legacy, not even on your radar?"

Jim took his own sweet time in coming up with an answer. "I would probably follow my heart. It's never let me down before."

Ash grunted. "Nothing but heartache down that path."

"Then you're not on the right path, son. Hey, look." He jumped from his chair in excitement and took the two steps to Ash. "You got one. You know what to do?"

"Dude, I'm a guy, of course, I do." He stared at the line. "Reel it in, right?"

"Let your line out a tad first. Get him good and hooked. That's it. Now, nice and slow bring him in."

The fish was no match for his novice ability, and within moments he hauled the lake monster through the hole. A tingle of pride puffed out his chest, and his whoop of triumph vibrated throughout the interior.

Jim shouted and slapped him on the shoulder. "Good job. You caught the first fish."

"My first fish."

"Your dad never took you fishing as a boy?"

"My dad didn't take me anywhere."

Jim took out his phone. "Hold it high and give me a smile. Let's mark this occasion."

"Can I keep it?" Ash asked after Jim snapped the photo. "I would like to cook it for dinner."

"Sure. I'd say he'd be a five, six-pounder."

An hour and a half later, Jim pulled into a parking space in front of the diner. After Ash caught his trophy fish, they'd tried for another hour to add to their stash, with no success. But their truce was stronger than ever.

Jim cleared his throat, cutting into Ash's thoughts. "I don't pretend to have all the answers. I wouldn't want to be in your place. But whatever it is, don't hurt Quinn. She doesn't need any more loss right now."

Ash hesitated, opened his mouth, but shut it again without saying a word. "Thanks for today," he said as he stepped from the car.

He had no intention of hurting Quinn. He also had no clue what a real relationship looked like.

Until now, he never cared.

Chapter Twenty-One

Quinn wiped the back of her hand across her forehead in frustration. Whoever said third time's a charm, lied. Four batches of cookies, all failures. And batch number five carried the same scent of impending disaster. She'd already wasted most of their supplies and not one edible morsel to show for all the hard work.

Amy had left a few minutes ago to make a store run and restock critical ingredients.

Flour turned her red apron white, and a thick layer coated her face and hair. She was elbow-deep in the bowl of dough when Ash strolled into the kitchen.

"Isn't this a beautiful sight?" A slow, sexy grin spread across his face and made the amber highlights in his eye glow.

Heat spread across her cheeks. "If you mean the cookies, don't get too excited."

"I mean, a woman dusted in flour with cookie dough on the side of her cheek."

Quinn's hand flew to her face. "What? Where?" She patted her face, but for every blob she knocked off another stuck.

Ash laughed. A rich, rumbling laugh that tingled clear down to her toes. "Here. Let me." He led her to the sink and turned on the water. Dampening a paper towel, he wiped away the evidence of her incompetence. He held her gaze a moment longer, then turned her around and plunged both their hands in the water.

Pinned between the cold metal of the sink and Ash's body heat, her insides rose and fell like a drop from the peak of a rollercoaster. She couldn't breathe as his hands slicked soap over her arms in a leisurely journey across every inch of flour-coated skin.

She licked her lips. Dear Lord, she'd never think of hand washing in the same light again.

"Quinn." Barney, the young cook helping her take the pans in and out of the oven, coughed.

Startled, they both jumped, splashing water droplets everywhere, and the neon sign of embarrassment burned out to her ears. Again. Ever since Ash walked through the door of Fisherman's Cottage, her face stayed in a permanent state of red. A tingle started between her shoulder blades and swept up the back of her neck to dance across her scalp. Maybe Barney hadn't noticed anything. Please, God. She turned in slow motion.

Judging by the ridiculous grin on the young man's face, luck was not on her side.

"Didn't mean to interrupt but, I don't think these are any better than the others." Barney held the tray out for their inspection.

"What in God's name are those? Mud pies?" Laughter laced Ash's voice.

"Chocolate chip cookies." She groaned. "That's the fifth batch. Amy is out getting more vanilla and sugar. I should have her get more flour, too."

"I'll text her," Barney said as he walked away, but he

stopped and glanced over his shoulder at them both with a cheesy grin. "As you were."

"Okay. That's it." She untied the strings of the apron from around her neck. "Done. Done. Done. I can't show my face in here ever again. I can't cook or bake, setting fire to the place, not my crowning achievement, and now this. Did you see the look Barney gave us? What did he think was going on over here?" She yanked the apron over her head, engulfing them both in a cloud of flour.

Ash coughed and waved his hand to clear the air. "Put that back on. You are not a quitter." His lips brushed her ear when he leaned in and lowered his voice for her alone. "And Barney knows exactly what was going on over here. Even if you don't."

Oh my gosh. The infuriating man found the whole thing funny.

He took her hand and led her back to the baking station. He shook the apron out before he put it around her neck.

"Oh no, you don't. I told you, I'm leaving." She whispered between her teeth, pushing the distasteful apron away.

"Darlin', you're making a scene. Is that what you want?" His breath tickled the hair around her face, and electrified chills danced over her skin.

The wicked man enjoyed every second of this. She cast a sheepish glance around the kitchen. Everyone gawked at them, and over in the corner, Barney whispered with Miguel, their teenage busboy.

She lowered her lashes and dropped her voice an octave above mute. "Wipe that silly grin off your face and give. Me. The. Apron." She snatched it from his hand and put it over her head, her movements short and jerky. Of all the infuriating men on the planet, Henrietta could've saddled her with, Ash Larsen was king.

"Why don't you start by telling me what these are?" Ash

picked up a cookie from the discard pile and banged it against the metal table. "Hockey puck? Cow patty?" He wrinkled his forehead as he flipped it over. "I got it, it's a doorstop?"

"Give me that." She made a grab for it and laughed when he pulled it away.

Instead, he dropped it back in the pile. "I hear tonight is a big deal. Jim said everything shuts down for the entire afternoon, and we haul everything over to Grand Marais for the party."

She nodded in agreement as she ran a wet cloth over the workspace.

"Then, why don't we get rid of this." He peered into the bowl. "I don't even know what to call it."

"Hey, no need to hurt my feelings."

"There are only so many mistakes you can make before we declare you incompetent in the baking arena," he joked.

Ash cleaned the bowl, and they started with a fresh batch of sugar cookies. He patiently showed her how to be exact in her measurements and took her through the process. "How is it you know nothing about baking or cooking?"

"All the stoves and ovens are gas-fired. I've never been able to go near the flame. It became a natural workaround." The ease with which she admitted that surprised her. Maybe the tears the other day had started the long-overdue healing process.

"Tell me about this party. Is this another tradition? It seems like Aunt Henrietta had a lot of them."

"It started before I came there. When Henrietta's father could no longer care for himself, she brought him up from St. Paul and put him in the retirement home in Grand Marais. One year, when he was too sick to leave for the day, she and Emerson took Christmas to him. It grew from there." She scooped a heaping cup of sugar and moved it to the bowl, but he stopped her.

"What in holy spit are you doing, woman? You trying to make me crazy?" He wrapped his hand around hers and moved it over the canister picking up a knife. "Baking is an exact science. Not a dump-and-run art form. No wonder we can't tell what those other things you call cookies are." He scrapped the knife across the top of the measuring cup and leveled the sugar.

She stifled a smirk. "That so?"

"Yea, that's so." He tossed the sugar into the bowl and reached for the butter.

Meanwhile, Quinn pulled the bag of flour toward her. "Hope Amy shows up soon. We only have enough for this one batch. I think."

"Step away from the white, powdery stuff. You still have to cream the sugar, butter, and vanilla together."

Amy came back from the store as the first successful batch of sugar cookies came out of the oven. Everyone in the kitchen cheered and high-fived. They called the kids staying at Fisherman's Cottage to decorate them.

"Don't you have appetizers to make?" Quinn asked.

"Got it covered. We made them last night in between orders, and I have Barney and Alissa working on the rest. I'm all yours, darlin'."

Both cooks had worked part-time with them for a few years and knew the drill. They would do an excellent job.

His hands moved like magic as he assembled the ingredients for the next recipe. She envied his ability to cook and bake.

Typically, she avoided the kitchen on baking day. Her job was to wrangle the kids and keep them decorating. With Carole Ann out and Ash off with Jim for the morning, she'd tried to step up and fill the void. She needed to quit doing that. It never ended well.

It was after three when they finished putting the last of the supplies into the truck. The food would go in when they were ready to leave.

"That's a wrap, everyone," Quinn said to the crew.

They all clapped, or fist-bumped their approval. It was a long day, but it had been fun.

"Go home. Rest up, and we'll see everyone back here in two hours." Quinn gave Amy a hug. "Thank you for all you did today."

"I did nothing." Amy nodded toward Ash. "I think you have a new protector." She shoved her hat down on her head. "See you tonight."

"You ready for the walk home? I heard it's snowing again." Ash shoved his hands in his pocket and offered her his elbow.

A girl could get used to this kind of attention.

Ash sat with one of the residents, Kevin Hogan, a feisty old gentleman who could talk the hide off a cow, with a zest for life that kept everyone around him on their toes.

After ten, many of the family members had already left. The crew they'd hired cleared the tables, taking all the leftovers to the center's refrigerator. The tree was up and decorated. He counted the party a success. One of the best parties he'd been too in a long time.

Funny, since his idea of a good time used to be hanging in a bar full of people who may or may not be his friends.

Tonight had been all about the residents of the retirement home. No live band. No dancing. Drinks consisted of alcohol-free punch. Chatting about grandkids was the main topic of conversation.

And Ash couldn't remember a better time.

"So, you're Henrietta's nephew. Lovely woman. She and

her husband used to come up here every month and spend time with everyone. We'll all miss her," Kevin said.

"Yes. I never met her, but she and my grandmother were twins."

Laughter floated across the room. Her laugh. Already familiar. Already sweet. Just like he knew how one curl refused to stay where she put it. The way her navy eyes turned a stormy gray when her emotions were high. And how she blushed the brightest pink when he teased her.

Quinn shifted to the right and put her glass on the table next to where she stood. The red dress she wore skimmed her body like a second skin, and three-inch heels brought her height to a whopping five foot three if she was lucky.

Many women dreamed of pulling off that look and failed. Quinn wore it with simple elegance. Tendrils of hair fell from the knot at the top of her head and brushed the long column of her neck and begged him to nuzzle until he found the pulse that jumped at the base.

She smiled at something her companion said, and his heart stuttered. Lightness filled the space in his chest. He raised his gaze and caught the cluster of evergreen and holly that dangled above her. He'd thought of little else since their first kiss in the moonlight. The sweetness of her lips as they parted to meet his own, kept him awake at night.

He put his own glass down and stood. "Excuse me, Kevin. I have to meet someone under the mistletoe."

The old man cackled with glee and shooed him on his way.

Ash had one mission. He allowed nothing or no one to stop him on the trek to the woman who occupied too many of his brain waves.

"Excuse me," he said as he stopped next to Quinn, extending his greeting to the woman she talked to. "Have you got a minute?"

"I'll let you two talk, my tired feet are ready to sit down for a rest. I've been standing the entire night."

"What's up?" Even with the three-inch heels, she needed to tilt her head to look at him.

"Darlin', you've left yourself exposed."

"I have? Why?" Startled, her eyes darted around.

He raised an eyebrow and pointed with his index finger.

She followed his gaze, and her mouth dropped when she glimpsed the mistletoe above her head. "Oh, no, no." She tried to step back, but he caught her.

Adrenaline rushed through his veins. "My sweet, Quinn, you of all people know the importance of traditions. You've been grilling me with them for weeks. I don't make the rules." He shrugged and lowered his voice. His finger traced the outline of her ripe, pink mouth. "I just follow them." Before she could utter another word of protest, he captured her lips in a hungry kiss.

When she melted into his arms, pleasure pulsed through him. She was all he wanted. All he could think about.

The gasps from the remaining group didn't faze them.

And neither did Amy's declaration. "Carole Ann's gonna hate she missed this."

They'd tumbled over the edge, and there would be no turning back.

Quinn climbed into bed and patted Niko on the head. She snuggled under the blankets and hugging the pillow to her chest, fluttered her feet. A silly grin had lurked beneath the surface all the way home from the party.

The kiss they'd shared under the mistletoe, for all the world to see, still burned through her. Lips still tingled with the taste of his. She tried to find sleep, but her mind raced. The longer Ash was here, the harder it was to imagine Elf Hollow without him.

Many more kisses like that and she'd be lost when he left.

Chapter Twenty-Two

Ash waited until Quinn left her cottage then he carried the rusty old trash can down to the lake. He'd found the gem the day before when taking the trash out to the dumpsters behind the diner. Before they'd left for the retirement center the night before, John had given him the keys to the garage and free rein to any tools he needed to convert the container into something usable.

Patches of rust disintegrated one side of the can and created the perfect niche for a skewer to go through while keeping the flames contained. All it needed was a bit of TLC to make it work for his purpose.

He tossed a few twigs in and started the fire. Barney would arrive any minute with food supplies from the diner. He'd tend the fire while Ash went in search of Quinn.

Now the million-dollar question. Could he get Quinn down here and, if he did, would she feel safe with the flames contained this way?

Barney meandered in a few minutes later loaded with a basket and a wide, toothy grin. "Amy called Carole Ann this morning and got her special hot chocolate recipe. I think you're gonna like it. Guaranteed to chase away the chills."

"Perfect." Couldn't hurt to ease some of her fear. "Pass along my thanks. Do you have everything for the S' mores?" He took the basket from Barney and flipped through the contents. That was the key to making all this work.

He found a Bluetooth speaker, blankets, skewers...Everything was there.

"You need to guard the fire until I get back."

"Sure thing, Ash, but I don't really think it will be a problem with all this snow on the ground."

The kid had a point. "Humor me then." Couldn't have a wild spark start a fire while he searched for Quinn.

He almost made it all the way into town before Quinn and Niko came into view. Sunlight danced through the strands of hair peeking from beneath her hat. The bulky down coat hid the body beneath. But that didn't stop his imagination from kicking into overdrive.

His fingertips still burned with the sensory memory of smooth satin skin. Seismic shifts of energy had rocked him since their shared kiss her under the mistletoe.

"Howdy," he said as he approached her.

Niko pranced and twirled a greeting, his leash a tangled mess around his legs by the time Ash knelt beside him.

"Ah, Niko, you need to at least pretend to be hard to get, boy." Ash chuckled as he grabbed the collar and unhooked the lead. "Here." He handed it to Quinn, "I'll hold him, you untangle the big brute." He scratched the dog behind the ears.

"You've made a friend for life," she said.

Once back on his leash, Niko fell into step between them both.

"Where have you been hiding? I haven't seen you all day." She tugged at an earlobe. An endearing habit she used when nervous.

"Would you like to see what I've been up to?"

"I need to get back and relieve Kylee."

"It's covered. Everyone is where they need to be, and I need you to follow me."

"Where are we going?"

"You'll see. Follow me."

An impish expression played across her face. "Ah, Ash, I hate to break it to you, but I know all about my cottage."

Ignoring her protests, he led the way onto the narrow path toward the shoreline. "Have patience, darlin'."

They stepped from the trees as Barney rushed out of sight.

The boy done good. He'd set everything out just as Ash instructed with the double-seater bench close enough to the fire for warmth, but far enough to keep Quinn's fear at bay. His playlist floated from the speakers, and the thermos of raspberry-flavored hot chocolate sat at the ready.

"What is all this?" She followed him into the clearing and stopped in her tracks. "You left a fire unattended?"

"No, Barney stayed. See?" He pointed to the kid's back as he retreated up the hill. "Now, you have nothing to worry about. I've planned out every last detail, everyone has been taken care of or assigned a task. You're off duty."

The sky-blue microfiber blanket snapped as he fluffed it and waited for her to sit on the folding love seat. When she didn't sit, he quirked a brow and leaned into her ear. "I don't bite, darlin'." He dropped his voice to a whisper.

Lips parted, breathing accelerated, but she took the seat.

"Amy sent Carole Ann's special cocoa, we have s' mores, music, and a sunset to watch." He poured the hot liquid from the thermos into a cup and passed it to her. The spice of chocolate and raspberries swirled in the steam between them. He settled into the seat next to her and draped the blanket over both their legs. Propped his feet on the log he'd put in place earlier.

"Ash, this is sweet. I don't even know what to say." The lines of her body visibly relaxed as she melted into his side.

His muscles jumped under the innocent grip of her hand. And heat seared through to the skin of his thigh like an ember from the fire. "Say, *Ash, you are the king of romance,* and we'll call it even." He couldn't hide the edgy need from his voice.

Cocoa sprayed from her mouth. A flirtatious flutter of her lashes followed. "Is that what this is?" She paused, "Romance?" Her gaze held him hostage, and the rosy tip of her tongue flicked across her lips.

Breath hissed from between his gritted teeth. Playful witch knew exactly the spell she cast. The power she wielded over him.

"Fine. I can live with simple obedience to my rules for the day." He took a sip of his drink, eager for a distraction. The velvety liquid coated his tongue in chocolate, and the warm raspberry liqueur spread through his limbs.

"I don't do obedience well. And certainly not open-ended."

"Here and now. That's it. Do you agree?" He counted on the fact she didn't like to back down on any challenge.

"Mm..." She eyed him up and down before she answered. "Fine. I think."

And she didn't disappoint.

He allowed her to relax into the moment. Let her enjoy the coca while they listened to music before he pounced.

"Let's make some s' mores," he announced. Not waiting for her reply, he pulled out the ingredients.

"I told you, I don't make them. But you go ahead." She tucked her legs under her and snuggled further under the blanket.

She was cute in a relaxed kitten-in-front-of-the-fire kinda

way. He *almost* hated to disturb her. But it was for her own good.

"Five minutes into our agreement, and you're already being a rebel." He yanked the blanket off them both and stood up. "I made this for you. See, it effectively contains the fire, no sparks to jump out at you, but you can get close enough it'll warm you." He held up the marshmallows. "And make s'mores."

She glared up at him. "Are you new here? You've seen first-hand what happens when I get near a fire. This is close enough right here. Thank you. But knock yourself out."

He'd hoped it wouldn't come to this, but he was prepared. "AHRR," he growled in the back of his throat. "Wrong answer, but thanks for playing. You can hate me later. However, you agreed to obey my rules."

"I thought you meant obedient in other ways." She wagged her eyebrows at him.

A ploy meant to distract him.

But, he liked the way her mind worked. Images began to unfold, sweet, beautiful ones. He shook his head to erase them before he could meander down that path. "Oh, no, you don't." He put one arm under her legs and the other behind her back and hauled her against his chest.

She squealed and grabbed onto his neck. "What are you doing?"

"Forcing compliance." He stood her behind the loveseat and moved it closer to the fire.

"If you think I'm going over there, you're wrong. Dead wrong." Her back stiffened, and she drew in a stuttered breath. She took first one then two steps back. Each move communicating her plan to bolt.

He ignored her, confident he could run her down if need be, and continued to pull out all the supplies and loaded marshmallows onto skewers. Then he stood to stalk his prey.

"No. Just no." She held her hand out.

As if that would stop him.

"Ash, I'm not kidding. I'm not doing this."

She made a run for it, but not before he caught her. He cradled her in his arms and carried her back to the chair. The tremors that racked her body broke his heart, and when she buried her face in his neck, he nearly called it quits. Instead, he tightened his grip and hoped it would end well.

He took the seat and settled her on his lap. "You can't spend the rest of your life terrified of candles. The only way to get over the fear is to face it. And there is no more delicious way than to make s' mores with a sexy hot guy willing to throw himself on a grenade for you."

She stiffened. "You'd do that?" A mixture of doubt and surprise laced her voice.

The comment was said in jest, something to lighten the mood. But *did* he mean it?

His heart faltered, enough the next breath died in his throat. "Yes, I'd do that. Now, will you roast a marshmallow? Please?" He held out one skewer and waited.

"Fine. On one condition."

"You already agreed to be obedient. Clearly not a strength," he grumbled.

A slight smile tugged at the corner of her mouth. "I'm amending the agreement. But I promise if you agree, I'll behave."

"Let me have it."

"I'll roast this marshmallow, but you have to answer any question I ask you."

"No."

"Then I'm done." She made a move to stand up, but he pulled her back.

"Agreed. Now take the darn stick."

The smug, satisfied look she gave him before squirming

around to face the fire made him instantly regret his statement.

"Snow covers the ground, and the fire is contained. It's safe," he said.

She sighed but reached a shaking arm toward the fire.

"Nice and slow."

The marshmallow tipped skewer slid into the space he'd created in the can.

"See? Nothing bad happened. Now all you do is wait." He locked his right arm around her waist and used his left hand to toast his own marshmallow. The smell of fresh rain filled his nostrils as her hair clouded around him.

"Mmm... This isn't bad. I can feel the heat, but it's not overwhelming." She turned a brilliant smile on him. "I've never made my own before."

"Well, you're in for a treat. Here, sandwich it between the two graham crackers and the square of chocolate."

She took a bite of the gooey prize, a contented expression on her face.

"How does it taste?"

"Heavenly." She held her stick out for him to load her up with another. "And don't look so pleased with yourself." Quinn heated the next one. "Just because I can sit encircled in your arms and put a stick in the fire doesn't mean I can go near a flame."

"But it's a first step."

"Why do you hate Christmas?"

Ice ran through his veins. "I don't hate it. But it's not my favorite holiday." Understatement of the year.

"You're splitting hairs. Why isn't it your favorite?"

He made his own sandwich before he answered. "I'm an open book."

A grunt pushed past her lips. "An open mystery book, maybe." She put her feet on the log and relaxed into his arm while enjoying her next creation. "You're a puzzle, Ash Larsen. I thought I had you all pegged, but these last couple of weeks..." Her voice faded, and she licked her fingers. "I don't know anymore. There is more to you than I first thought."

"I agreed to one question, and you already asked."

"No, I said, you have to answer *any* question I ask you."

She did not understand what it would cost him to answer that question. He kept all those answers locked deep in a cool dark place where they wouldn't hurt.

"If my father had his way, I wouldn't be here. And almost every Christmas, he got to pretend I wasn't. He and Eric would go on a trip. I stayed behind with a nanny."

"But why would he do that?" She twisted in his lap, her legs draped over the arm of the chair.

The sun sank lower in the sky, the last of its warmth drained with it. How to answer that without sounding like a loser? "My father had one true love. The way I heard it, he and my mother were inseparable. Gran used to say my mother brought out everything good in him. And when she died, she took all the virtue with her. At least when it comes to me."

A hollowness settled in his chest, he swallowed to dislodge it. "She died in the hospital. A few hours after I was born. A blood clot got to her lungs. My father has never forgiven me for that."

Quinn pulled off her gloves and dropped them in her lap. Cold fingers curled around his neck, drew his head forward until their foreheads touched. "I'm sorry you grew up without a mother to comfort you. You grew up without a father, too. You didn't deserve that. He had no right. Your father sounds like a troubled man."

"When I was younger, I did everything I could to earn his love. Eventually, I learned nothing would be good enough. I stopped. Instead, I came up with ways to get under his skin." *Yeah, you're a freakin' pro at pissing the old man off.*

181

Perfect by Ed Sheeran came on, and Quinn jumped to her feet.

"Dance with me." Poised in front of him, holding his hands, she was oblivious to the fire inches away.

"Here? In the snow?"

"Please. I love this song."

He could deny her nothing.

She reached up and twined her arms around his neck.

He hesitated a split-second before he placed his hands at her waist and pulled her as close as their puffy coats would allow.

"Thank you for this. The s' mores, the fire, the dance."

"You're welcome." Ash knew, in that moment, he'd found a woman he could come home to.

Purple and pink and fading light weaved in and out of clouds as the last of the sun's rays echoed across the sky.

Quinn rested her cheek on Ash's shoulder, her mind racing at the same speed as her heart. Too fast. *Breathe, Quinn.*

Confusion screamed at her. She thought she'd pegged him the minute he walked in her door. But now she didn't know. The s' mores, the fire, the planning, dancing in the snow when he didn't like the cold. He knew how she took her coffee. These were not the acts of a self-centered playboy.

The song had ended, and they continued to sway, locked together in a timeless embrace. Her heart hurt to think of the hatred his father had for him. He'd spent a lifetime building a mask, and tonight he showed her the man behind the careful construction. Something she didn't take lightly.

Later as they walked back to her cottage, the full moon

hung low in the sky, large and bright, but that's not what caught her eye. She stopped and pointed to the sky. "Look."

Swirls of blue and hues of pink and green danced and rolled against the ink-black sky.

"Is that the aurora borealis?" Awe tinged his voice.

"It is. And the moon is almost full. It'll be full by Christmas. A Christmas moon."

Magical.

Ash pulled her into a tight embrace and rested his chin on her head. "I've never shared anything like this with anyone, Quinn. I want you to know how special tonight was."

Chapter Twenty-Three

Quinn flipped over to her back and stared wide-eyed at the ceiling. She'd been tossing and turning since two o'clock. It was now; she picked up her phone, four a.m. Longest. Night. Ever.

Kicking her feet, she pulled the pillow over her face and groaned.

The mattress drooped when Niko climbed onto the bed next to her, nudging his nose under her arm. She laughed and hugged him. "I'm okay, you big ball of fur."

Restlessness plagued her since Ash left. Her mind kept going to the s' mores, the dance. His story. Her chest ached at his confession. How could a father be that cruel? She needed to talk to someone, anyone. She glanced at her phone. Managed to kill fifteen minutes. She marked the hours until society deemed it acceptable to intrude on Carole Ann.

"Enough," she snapped and booted her feet free of the heavy blankets. She pushed herself from the bed, pulled on a cardigan, and shuffled into the kitchen. She grabbed a glass of milk from the fridge, picked up the box of letters from Henrietta's sister, and headed for the couch. Niko materialized at her side, annoyance on his puppy face at being disturbed. "I'm sorry, but I can't sleep. No one said you had to get up, too." She shivered and pulled the blanket off the back of the couch and eyed the gas fireplace. She'd convinced Henrietta to switch all the old log fireplaces to gas a few years back, and she'd insisted they convert Quinn's at the same time. Quinn tried to tell her it would be a waste, but Henrietta wouldn't listen.

As she sat there shivering in the wee hours, she couldn't help but remember the glorious warmth that emanated from the fire earlier. All it would take is a mustard seed of strength and a bit of backbone to turn on the flame of the fireplace. She rose and crossed the floor to the hearth, her hand hovered over the switch. The glass was there to prevent accidents. No more fear. She flipped it before she could stop herself. The flame leaped to life, and her heart somersaulted in her chest. One, then two steps back, her breath refused to normalize, but fear would no longer rule her. Ash believed in her.

She sat back down and picked up a letter to take her mind off the fire and lost herself in the pages. Three hours passed in a blink. She had learned nothing earth-shattering in the batch of writing, but she loved the connections and the stories she read about Ash and Eric when they were young. Ash's grandmother worried about him in every letter. The lack of parental love was at the top of her list.

A couple hours later, she pulled into the driveway at Carole Ann's house outside town. Grabbing the bag of breakfast from the seat next to her, she made her way to the door. Carole Ann's husband told her he'd leave the door unlocked.

"Hello. I've come bearing food."

"Back here," Carole Ann shouted. "And I'm hungry."

Quinn followed the sound of her voice to the back of the house and entered a cozy family room. A cheerful fire crackled in the fireplace. She hesitated for a split second outside the doorway.

"Sorry, sunshine. Alex started it for me before you called."

"That's okay. I'm fine." She ran fingers through her hair and took a deep, steadying breath before she approached her friend and gave her the food. "How you doing?"

Carole Ann's left leg was in a cast from her ankle to her hip. Broken in three places, she had to have pins surgically placed. "I'm better. I'm down to two pain pills a day and one at night. But I'm tired of being confined to the house."

"I bet. You're involved in everything. It's got to be making you crazy."

"Alex has been a huge help. He's had to finish my Christmas shopping. And the kids are back until after the holidays. I'm a happy mama." She peeked inside the bag. "Is this the new breakfast sandwich Ash makes? I've heard a lot of good things."

"It is. I have no idea what he puts in those eggs, but it's a hit."

Carole Ann took a bite and licked her lips. "Oh my God, that's heaven. I heard he was a master."

Quinn dug into her own. She waited until they were both done before broached what she came for.

"What's on your mind?"

"Is it that obvious?"

"I know when something's on your mind. Is everything okay at the diner?"

"It's great. Ash has stepped in and taken over everything..." Her words penetrated. "I'm sorry, I didn't mean it like that."

"Oh, stop. It's all good. Ash is a trained chef, and I'm a woman who likes to cook. Henrietta paid me for years to do what I love. Now, why don't you fill me in."

Quinn shared the night before with her and held nothing back. Except for Ash's secret. "I can't believe he went to all the trouble, converting the trash can, setting it up. I stood so close, sweat beaded beneath my coat. The whole thing terrified me, but I had no doubt Ash would keep me safe."

"Doesn't sound like you have the same opinion of the man you did a few weeks ago."

"I don't know. I thought I had him pegged. Another Ty. Cocky, pompous, self-centered. But now I'm not sure."

"You judge every datable man you meet by Ty's standards, you've set the bar low."

"That's not true. I've been on lots of dates since I came back. Not everybody is a Ty. I know that."

Carole Ann stared in the fire. "You've dated Sam from the bank, you've dated Rocky from the tree farm, Jack from the retirement center. All safe, secure, men."

"Want's wrong with that?"

"One could almost say *boring.*"

"That is not very nice. They're good men."

"Yes, and safe. They are not a risk. And you are not interested in any of them, or you'd still be dating one. They do not spark your interest."

"But what if I'm wrong about him? What if Ash is exactly who I thought he was? What if he convinces his brother to sell to the ski resort? They'll own one-half. I don't know if I can fight that."

"And what if he's not? Give him a chance, Quinn. Let him fail you before you invent a reason or let him prove he's everything you deserve. Either way, live. This is what Henrietta feared."

Exasperated, Quinn stood and grabbed her bag, and Carole Ann's and took them to the kitchen trash can. She took her time coming back. "Did Henri share that with everyone? Helen told me the same thing the night of the tree party."

"She loved you. That's what happens. She didn't want you to use her death and the company as an excuse not to find someone until it was too late."

Quinn stared out the back window. Three blue jays battled over the birdseed hanging from the rope off the eaves.

Was she so predictable that everyone knew before she did who she would turn away? Images from the night before rippled through her. Held in the circle of his arms, the spicy scent of him mingled with the smoke from the fire. His hurt was real. She knew it.

He knew how to make her coffee to perfection. He danced in the snow. The man who hated the cold danced three slow songs in the snow.

For her.

Was it enough? It would have to be.

For now.

Chapter Twenty-Four

A sh's phone rang, and he picked up without checking to see who it was. Big mistake.

"About darn time, you took my call." Eric's angry voice greeted him.

He wasn't ready for this conversation. Then again, he would never be prepared. "Hey, can I call you back? I'm headed out the door." Quinn waited for him at the cottage, and he chomped at the bit to get to her. The last thing he wanted to do was waste time dealing with Eric.

"Where would you be going at ten o'clock at night in deadsville? Never mind. You've been avoiding my calls since you quit a week ago. I got you, I'm not letting you go that easily." A mixture of annoyance and concern laced Eric's tone.

"What is so important that it can't wait?" Ash snapped.

"All right then, right to the point. Why did you quit?"

Ash weighed his words. He and Eric were close, but Eric and their father were thick as fleas on a hound dog. Did he trust his brother? "I should've done this years ago." And he meant it. He still hadn't figured out where he went from here, but he'd dumped a lot of baggage with that one move.

"But all you did is play into the old man's hands. Why make it easy for him? Granddad made it clear he could never fire you."

A flush of heat volleyed through him, and his stomach hollowed as if someone had punched him. "You were part of that?" The number of secrets kept by this family astounded him. Starting with his grandparents' *entire* lives and ending with this. What other nuggets did Eric have privy to?

"Not until the other week after I talked to you. For what it's worth, I'm sure Granddad meant well."

Why is it everyone in his life meant well, but it never worked in his favor? Gran, Granddad, Henrietta. "You don't get it. The fact he had to tie dad's hands to keep me employed..." Ash's voice trailed off.

There'd always been that one blade of hope the old man kept him around because deep down, he loved him. That blade was currently buried hilt deep in his back.

"I'm sorry." Eric sighed. "What are you going to do now? You have no job. Based on your history, I'm gonna go out on a limb and assume the marriage trust fund isn't going anywhere for you. You've banked everything on what's happening up there. I sure hope you realize what you're doing."

He glanced out the window and scratched his neck. The view offered one of two scenic images depending on the time of day. A dazzling white so brilliant it burned the eyes or silvery-gray by moonlight. With shades of one or the other thrown in for flavor.

Did he know what he was doing?

"Speaking of which, any progress?" Eric broke through Ash's thoughts.

Restless, he left his supplies on the counter and wandered out the back door. The stab of piercing air washed through him, cleared his mind as if somehow, the frigid temperatures had the power to cleanse his soul. Warmth bloomed in his chest as he scanned the mountains surrounding the lake. Striking and dramatic. Startled at the thought, he stopped mid-step. When had this town become anything but cold and miserable?

"Things have changed, Eric. At least I think they have."

Eric groaned. "Please don't tell me you've succumbed to all the hometown sentimentality. Christmas, small towns, you don't even like that stuff."

"It's different here. I'm different. Everyone knows your business before you do. And they care about you." He exhaled. Molecules of moisture became specks of ice crystals suspended in the air.

"And you *like* that? You don't even like it when the family knows you sneeze. Geez, Ash, what the heck happened after I left?"

"It's complicated."

"It's Quinn, isn't it?" Disbelief edged Eric's voice. "I'll be darned."

"Aww, knock it off, Eric." Ash scoffed and took a deep breath.

"She cracked through that cage you built. She's smart as a hoot owl and cute as a calico kitten at Easter. But not your usual type."

"Let's get real. None of that changes anything. I don't deserve someone like her."

"No. She's *exactly* who you need. You're the only one who thinks you don't. Darn it, Ash, when are you going to let go of all that anger and live your life? I get it, Dad treated you like crap. But you're free of him now. You got Quinn, Gran's trust fund, and when we sell, you'll have Henrietta's inheritance. Let it go."

Ash went back into the house to finish rounding up the supplies to take to Quinn's. "They're good people, Eric. With families and lives. Henrietta and Emerson built something amazing here."

"All the more reason to sell to the ski resort. They'll come in and turn Elf Hollow around. Give the economy the boost it needs. Quinn will thank you in the long run."

Ash had held the same opinion when he'd first arrived. But thanks to Henrietta, he knew better. Elf Hollow didn't need a turnaround. "You'd be wrong on that count. Quinn will not thank us for selling and leaving her to deal with the resort."

"I'm going to give you some advice. Everyone has a story, Ash. Pain filled and ugly. Some more than others. But pain teaches you how to live your life. You can be bitter, or you can grow. Way I see it, you've been walking around with a whole lot of bitter. Maybe it's time to toss it out for something better."

"Yeah? What if there isn't anything better?"

"Quit making things difficult. Do you love her?"

Ash paused. The question raced around his head. Did he? He sighed and scrubbed his face. "I wouldn't recognize love if it stood naked before me."

"Love makes your heart race, and your chest hurt until you can't breathe. You count the seconds until you see them again, and you'd do anything to see them smile. Nothing else matters."

"Is that how it was for you and Lizzy?" Ash asked.

"Still is. Every day."

His breath stilled.

"Is she someone you could come home to every night?" Eric asked.

He thought back to the start of the phone call. How antsy he'd been to get to Quinn. How her smile jump-started his day. A jumble of emotions battered him like a hurricane lashing at a seawall.

Ah, really? He was in love. And that complicated everything.

"I'll take your silence as a yes. Congratulations are in order. I have to admit, Dad didn't think you had it in you. I never doubted you. How long after you're married do you think it will take her to agree to sell?"

Ten days past never. "I have to go. Quinn's waiting for me."

A few minutes later, Ash navigated the moonlit path to Quinn's cottage, a bag of groceries tucked under his arm. The brilliance of the Aurora Borealis from the night before was now notably absent from the sky. He kept replaying the phone call with Eric over and over in his head, testing the validity of the revelation.

When Quinn came to the diner earlier and asked him to dinner at her place after he closed, he'd been surprised. But pleasantly so.

The memory of their dance beneath the stars would be forever engraved on his brain. The scent of fresh rain, Quinn's signature scent, a cloud around them.

He'd found himself whistling throughout the day, a spring in his step.

Niko barked the second his boot hit the porch. A chuckle shook through him. Dog. Man's best alarm system.

"Niko, you'll wake the dead. Hush."

His chest tightened when Quinn's playful tone floated out the door seconds before she opened it. Any air left in his lungs gushed from him in one long exhale. The vision she offered, framed expectantly in the doorway, hair flowing down her back, fired off sensory neurons inside him like sparklers on the Fourth of July.

Chest tight. *Check.* Couldn't inhale if he wanted to. *Check.* And a smile sweet as honey fresh from the hive. *Check.*

"Ash," she said, her voice, breathless.

Petite, beautiful, pure. There was no pretense to Quinn. Dressed in a purple sweater that fell off one shoulder, worn jeans, and thick socks, she was innocence. An innocence that shouldn't be tainted by the likes of him.

And yet here he stood. A foolish grin written across his face and, try as he might, he couldn't wipe it off. "Howdy."

"Come in. What did you bring?" She took the bag to the kitchen and left him to remove his coat and boots.

"Rummaging around the kitchen at the main house the other day, I found a blast from the past. Fondue pot." He came into the living room.

Struck by one word. Inviting. Like coming home. Over-stuffed off white couch and chair with bright orange and pink pillows filled most of the space. Simple black and white pictures with a splash of color filled one entire wall and lamps added a warm glow. He turned when a wave of heat hit his back. "You turned on the fire," he shouted as he took the few steps to the kitchen. His hands gripped her upper arm to steady her when they collided.

"I still can't go near it. It's silly. It's behind glass, but I flip the switch and run. I turned it on this morning, too." The way her gaze flickered shyly tugged at his heart.

He ran a finger along her jawline and tipped her chin up. "Yesterday, you couldn't turn it on. Baby steps." He gave her nose a playful tap. "Let's make dinner. I'm starving." He dropped his arm over her shoulder and led her back to the kitchen. He wanted to kiss those sweet lips, but it was too soon. Take it slow. "I have a day-old baguette, a stick of pepperoni, a hunk of ham, and some veggies." He pulled things out of the bags and handed them to her.

"I've never had fondue. What goes in it?"

"Traditionally, you would melt everything in the pot over

a flame, but that takes too long. I'm going to put the pot on the stovetop and then transfer it to the Sterno."

"Wait. Sterno. That's an open flame." Her teeth nibbled at her lower lip, and her pupils widened, swallowing the color.

"A wee flame, there won't be any heat coming from it. And I'm going to melt it all while you stand right over there and cut everything into nice rustic chunks." He pulled out a knife, handed her all the food, and steered her to the other side of the counter.

"And the wine." Ash opened the bottle then pulled out two glasses.

After pouring them each a class, he added a big splash to the double boiler and turned the gas on low. While the wine came up to heat, he grated the gruyere and gouda, then he cut the brie into small bits and chopped the shallots. Once the wine warmed, he mixed all the ingredients together.

After it was all melted, he moved the melted goodness to the Sterno rack on the table and handed her two fondue forks. "The flame is puny. You can hardly call it a flame, and you won't feel it. I promise. Pick your hunk of choice— bread, veggie or meat— and dip in the sauce."

She jabbed a hunk of bread and a thick slice of pepperoni and swirled it through the sauce. White, gooey cheese hung from the end of the fork and stuck to the corner of her mouth as she tried to catch it all in one bite.

"You got something, right there." He reached across the table, cupped her chin, and thumbed the cheese away. Time stopped. Her face flushed, and the tip of her tongue traced across her bottom lip. Velvety, kissable lips.

When she turned away, he dropped his hand. He had it bad.

"I took Carole Ann one of your breakfast sandwiches this morning. You impressed her."

"Didn't upset her, did it? I mean, I don't want to step on her toes."

"She doesn't care about that kind of thing. She's thrilled you're here to take over."

They finished eating and took their wine to the couch. Before he could stop himself, he pulled her under his arm, their bodies pressed together. "Last night was...." He was at a loss for words.

"Yeah, me, too. Very much."

He laced his fingers through her hair, his thumb tracing the arch of her brow. He kissed the closed lid of each eye. "Thank you for yesterday."

"You did it all. The fire, the S' mores, the dance." She grabbed his hand and brought it to her mouth, pressing a soft kiss in the palm.

"I need to tell you something. But, I'm not sure how to do this." His muscles twitched beneath skin stretched tight as a bloated tick. "My relationships don't last past three weeks. I'm not built that way, I guess. But these last few weeks, with you, here..." He made a move to stand. "You deserve better. I'm not good at this."

She grabbed his arm and pulled him back to the couch. "Don't stop." Her gaze caught and held his, her face radiant.

"I've never wanted to be with someone for the simple pleasure of being with them. No strings, no ulterior motives, no pretense. I've never longed for someone's smile because I can't breathe without it. Do you know how that feels?"

Her head barely moved in acknowledgment.

His heart pounded in his throat. He couldn't make eye contact with her. Instead, he played with the silky tendrils framing her face. "I'm mucking this up, but what I'm trying to say is... I love you, Quinn."

All his experience with women hadn't prepared him for this. One side glance from her and he was reduced to a twelve-year-old boy stumbling over his words asking a twelve-year-old girl for his first date. Palms sweaty, nerve endings sparking like a live wire, he wanted to run.

Her jaw went slack, and her eyebrow shot to her hairline. "Ash?" She whispered. "Do you mean that?"

Words eluded him, so he answered her in the only way he could. With a kiss, and not some gentle peck. All his bottled-up emotions and feelings and desires poured out of him into that one, mind-altering kiss. He gave her everything he had to give.

His reward came when she yielded and melted into him, her arms twined around his neck. The warmth from her body filled his arms, rippled to the icy place in his chest.

"I love you, too." She curled into his lap, and his hands encircled her waist.

His heart jackhammered against his ribs so hard he knew they would crack. Running his hands down the sleek curve of her back, he nuzzled the pulse at the juncture of her neck and collar bone. Supple contours yielded beneath his touch, and a beautiful moan rumbled in her throat.

He could spend the rest of his days right here on this couch with her and never regret a moment.

Chapter Twenty-Five

Quinn trembled. A tendril of hope burst to the surface, like the first crocus of spring pushing through the snow. She leaned into him, fitting their bodies together like a puzzle, long, firm fingers kneaded the back of her arm, commanding, self-assured, and all male.

She broke away and caressed the lines of sorrow and loneliness he'd been holding inside for too long. What kind of father would be so bitter and heartless to his own son? Her stomach knotted. Ash could've easily turned out the way she first viewed him, a callous, self-centered jerk. "You expect me to believe you've never dated someone longer than three weeks?" She pulled back and waited for him to answer.

"Rule number one. Never date them past three weeks." His arms tightened, and his forehead rested on hers. "But all that is about to change."

Quinn smoothed the shirt down the brick wall he called a chest. "You have rules?" A prickly sensation zipped across her scalp.

"Doesn't everyone?"

"I suppose we do."

Niko picked that moment to jump onto the couch and howl for attention.

A deep laugh burst from Ash, and she pressed a hand to her mouth to stifle her giggles.

"He needs out. Don't move."

"I'll take him. I should leave anyway."

"What? Already?"

"Trust me, I *need* to go." A long, slow kiss later, and he stood up with her cradled in his arms and dropped her onto the chair. A lazy grin curled his yummy lips, and he stretched like a cat in a pool of sunshine.

She loved his smile. The dimple that sat at the corner of his mouth. "You're like chocolate, I can never stop at one piece."

He put his boots and coat on and grabbed Niko's leash. "Come on, boy, let's go."

She bounced on her toes as she greeted them at the door a few minutes later.

He didn't take off his coat. Instead, he pulled her into a hug. "Coffee in the morning?"

"Count on it." She shut and locked the door behind him, her body a restless ache of longing.

She flipped out the lights as she hummed her way to the bedroom, breathlessness making her steps light. Even Niko trotted with a happy grin. After completing her nighttime routine, she crawled into bed. Thoughts zipped through her head, flicking from one to the other fast as lighting. Too keyed up to sleep, she turned the tv on with the volume low.

Helen's comments, the night of the tree decorating, popped into her head. If she was right, and Henrietta played one last round of matchmaking, she did an exceptional job. Ash was everything she'd ever dreamed of. Tall, handsome, thoughtful, generous, and sweet.

Needing a distraction, she pulled the shoebox full of

letters onto the bed and rifled through them. The letters had become a bedtime story of sorts and a ritual. She selected an envelope from the stack of unread messages and plumped her pillow before snuggling down to read.

My dear Henny-Penny,

I fear this may be one of the last letters you'll receive from me.

My health is failing. My doctors give no hope.

It's the cancer. I'm ready. My life did not go as I planned, but then

neither did yours, I guess. I have only myself to blame for my pain and yours.

Many people have had to pay for my one night of

indiscretion. The good news is I've had the time to put my affairs

in order. The bad news, I had to make a difficult decision. I love my

sweet Ash dearly. He is the light of my life, but I can't abide by his

life choices. He is irresponsible and refuses to accept love. I've tied

his inheritance into a trust fund that can only be accessed if he marries

and settles down. It is a move I fear he will hate me for, but it's

for his own good. I pray he and you will forgive me my mistakes.

It is with great sadness I bid you goodbye.

Unease rolled through Quinn like a chilled, dark fog off the lake. She reread the words. Tremors shook her hands, and the walls shifted closer, suffocating. Words blended and blurred into one massive inkblot, and she dropped the letter into her lap.

Tears pooled in her eyes. Her mind was a big, black hole of

nothing as if someone came in and dumped it all out. She couldn't focus. Her hand flew to her mouth, and she jumped out of bed. "Oh, god, it's Ty all over again." She moaned into the empty room.

Her mind played over the last few weeks, the previous three days.

She wrapped her arms around herself and rubbed the cold from her skin. No. No. She couldn't be wrong. Not again.

Then why did he make a beeline for the door as soon as she admitted her love?

A cringe-worthy memory reared its ugly head. The moment she'd bounced in the doorway with excitement, waiting for him to come back in with Niko.

She dropped her head into her hands and sent out a silent plea. *Please, God, don't let this be another humiliation.* The cost would be so much higher than before.

At precisely six a.m., Quinn and Niko jogged up the steps to Amy's apartment. Lack of sleep took its toll, and with each blink, her eyelids scraped like an emery board over the corneas. A throb of pain pounded in sync with an erratic heartbeat at her temples. Tossing and turning most of the night left her restless, anxious, and in need of SOS time with Amy.

It was early, but she had complete confidence her best friend would be waiting for her. Amy might stay up with the owls, but she rose with the sun no matter what time she went to bed.

Quinn pounded on the door. "Amy, it's me. Open up. It's cold out here."

The door opened before Quinn finished her sentence. "Darn right, it's cold. Get your butt in here." Amy grabbed Quinn's coat and hauled her in the door. "Merry Christmas Eve."

Quinn gave her a blank stare. She forgot it was the twenty-fourth.

"Are you all right?" Concern etched across Amy's forehead.

"Maybe. Yes. I don't know."

The SOS grew from two angsty teenage girls in eighth grade with a melodramatic sense of injustice. They only used it in the most desperate circumstances. Family trouble, teacher trouble and, the most important point, boy trouble. The last time Quinn had invoked the SOS was the night she'd discovered Ty in bed with another woman. She stayed on the phone with Quinn all through the night. Until Quinn fell asleep under her vow to not allow jerks in her life ever again.

"Coffee?" Quinn asked as she suppressed a shiver.

"Yup, all ready to go. I have my cup. Get yours while I settle Niko with water, and I'll meet you in the living room." Amy took off his leash and led him into the kitchen.

Quinn hung up her coat and toed off her boots. Once Niko found his toy and a spot to plop and they had their coffee, they convened on the couch.

"Spill it. What's up that you had to invade my sacred morning routine?" Amy asked with a playful grin.

Quinn took a deep, steady breath. During the walk over, she'd pondered the best way to broach the subject, still didn't have a clue. "Ash, said he loved me last night," she gushed in one long exhale. Like pulling off a bandage. Quick and painless. But with more pain.

"What? And you waited this long to tell me? What did he say? What did *you* say?" Amy flipped her whole body around and sat crossed legged facing Quinn. A grin as wide as Lake Superior cut across her face. "Tell me everything."

Quinn nibbled on her thumbnail. "I told him I love him, too."

Amy squealed and kicked her feet. "I knew it. I felt it the first time I saw you two together. All the way down deep, ya feel me? Right here." Her hand fisted at her stomach for emphasis. "I love it when I'm right. Wait." She cocked her head and stared at Quinn. "You have the same expression as the time Jonas Cooper got up on stage at the tenth-grade talent show and sang a song he wrote for you. It's your deer-in-headlights, happy-dance, look. I hate that look. I'm never sure if we're celebrating or terrified."

"Both?"

Amy's gaze penetrated deep into Quinn's and understood, as only a best friend can, there was more to the story. "I get the happy-dance. Why are you as white as the backside of a snowshoe rabbit?"

Quinn tugged at her ear, struggling for comfort where she feared there may be none. No, she wouldn't consider that. This was different. Ash was different.

"I found this after he left." She handed Amy the letter from Sadie. "It's out of the box the attorney gave us. I read a few every night before I fall asleep. They're filled with tons of information. The story behind Henrietta and Sadie, getting a glimpse into the boy Ash used to be." She bit her lip.

Would the lonely boy Sadie wrote about, the one who longed for love and acceptance, grow up to become the worst kind of player? She shook her head, dismissing the dark thought before it could gain traction.

After reading the letters, it wasn't hard to understand why Ash hated Christmas. His father had left him to his own devices year after year.

Amy read the letter several times before she glanced up. Even white teeth worried the corner of her lower lip, and twin furrows dug into the space between her eyes. "Did he ever mention this to you?"

"No, but it's not like it's the kind of thing people talk about. *Hey, by the way, how do you get access to your trust fund? Mine's tied up until I marry.* I've never even known anyone with a trust fund." Her sharp tone stopped Niko mid-squeak on his toy, his manner alert.

"Perhaps Henri wanted you to find this?"

Quinn jumped up and paced. "Why give me the whole box? Why not give me this one? There are a lot of letters. Ash took a handful. He could have gotten this one and destroyed it before I ever saw it. As plans go --" she threw her hands up in defeat, "-- not well thought out."

"Maybe she forgot it was in there." Amy offered.

"Possible." Quinn conceded. "But why go to all this trouble?"

"She saw how devastated you were when Ty..." Amy trailed off as if searching for the right words. "When it ended the way it did. Maybe this was her way of warning you not to trust Ash."

"All Henri knew was that I broke it off with him. I never told her what details."

Amy raised an eyebrow in question.

"What?"

"You might not have told her all the parts, but she wasn't blind. All of us saw how hurt you were."

So much for keeping a secret. She slouched, her chin hitting her chest. "It's all confusing. Were you aware that Henri and Emerson had a hobby? They liked to play match-maker. They hooked up Jim and Ally. Helen said they brought her and Sam together. And she mentioned a couple of other guests they'd introduced over the years. Helen seemed to think I was Henri's next project."

Neither of them spoke as they processed the information.

Amy was the first to speak. "Now that you've mentioned it, it kinda makes sense. About six months after you came home, Henri started asking me questions about you. She's good. Until now, I hadn't given it much thought."

"What kinds of questions?" Quinn asked.

"Like, what types of movies we go too, what men interested you—"

"She knew all that."

"Yes, from the perspective of a parent or grandparent. Not my perspective. She wanted to figure out what made you, *you*."

Quinn toppled onto the couch and stretched her feet onto the coffee table. "What? She researches me, talks to Sadie? They decide to hook Ash and me up, and then Henrietta has second thoughts and wants me to find the letter? Arg!" She dropped her head back and stared at the ceiling. "I don't know what to believe."

Amy smoothed a hand over her leg. "Did you ever stop to think that she didn't let the trust fund marriage thing bother her because she thought you guys were right for each other? Did he say what he planned to do with his share of the inheritance?"

Quinn's stomach dropped to her feet. She'd never even considered that. "No, but I guess I assumed after all that..." Her voice faded away, the taste of misery too heavy on her tongue to continue.

"How do you feel about him?" Amy asked.

Quinn had no hesitation. His smile was a shot of espresso in her morning. He took the time to figure out her fear and how to help her overcome it. He shared his past, something personal and private. Painful. He'd built a bond between them. Regardless of his motive, she'd already given him her heart.

"I love him."

"Then you have to talk to him. You have to find out if he knew about this."

"He knows. How could he not? Sadie died over a year ago." Niko nuzzled Quinn's leg, and she obediently rubbed the fur around his collar.

"I see him at the diner every day, and he seems happy. I mean, like, whistling-while-walking-on-a-cloud kinda happy. He's making menus, experimenting with new foods, humming. Everyone loves him," Amy said.

Including me. A chill touched the base of her spine and spiraled all the way to her scalp. But no one else would end up with a broken heart if this turned out to be nothing more than a ploy to get her to drop her guard.

Amy sighed and handed her the letter. "You gotta talk to him."

After she dragged out the walk back to the B&B as long as she could, she paced the sidewalk outside the house. She needed a plan. She couldn't approach someone and say, is it true you have a trust fund? Or perhaps it should go something like, are you marrying me for your money? She snorted. That would be funny if not so real and raw.

She dropped to the porch step. Niko sat between her knees, where she buried her face in his cold fur and hugged him. "What do I do, Niko? It's already too late."

Standing, she took a deep breath and climbed the last of the stairs. A tentative smile curled her lips. If she was going to fool the breakfast crowd, she needed to do better than that. Squaring her shoulders, she brightened, opened the door, and stepped through the doorway.

Chapter Twenty-Six

"Ash, this is about the best breakfast I've ever eaten. It topped yesterday," Brad, one of the guests said.

His wife, Gemma, threw her napkin at his face. "Wow. Thanks. My mornings just got better. You've had your last eggs al a Gemma, buster."

Everyone at the table laughed and joined in the compliments. Ash couldn't help the swell of pride that drifted through him. He'd taken over all of Carole Ann's duties, both in the diner and here in the B&B.

Cooking was the love he didn't know he had until he stumbled upon it, and to hear these people rave about his talent, was the acceptance he'd always craved. Hopefully, critic reviews would be as glowing when his restaurant opened.

"Can I get anyone anything else? I have a few more waffles left and some muffins." Baking was not his favorite, but he could make it work.

The front door opened, and Quinn and Niko came in covered with snow. She temporarily froze when their gazes met across the room. And then she recovered. So slight, no one else would even notice.

Coming into the dining room, she grinned at everyone. "Merry Christmas Eve!"

"Merry Christmas, Ms. Quinn!" All the kids chimed at once from the kids' corner. The adults all greeted her, as well.

Ash pulled out a chair for her and began to fix a plate. "Oh, I'm good. Thanks. I grabbed something from the diner while Niko and I were out for our walk. Lots of work to get done before tonight."

"Oh, dear, please. You've worked yourself too much. We've hardly seen you this year," Helen said as she patted the seat Ash held for her.

"Well, maybe some coffee."

"I'll get it," Ash offered. He kept his ear on the conversation as he made her mug the way she liked it. He couldn't put his finger on it, but there was something off. Almost too forced and perky.

"Here you go."

"Thanks."

Ash made himself a cup and pulled up a chair next to her. He touched her hand under the table, and she jumped.

The conversation flowed, but slowly the families gathered their children and started their day.

Everyone but Helen and Sam had left.

"Ash, I must say. You've brought a lot to this holiday. It's been nice to see you and get to know you. I think Henri and Emerson would have enjoyed you. Don't you, dear?" She turned to her husband.

"Indeed. It's too bad they didn't get the chance to meet you," Sam offered.

"Thank you. It's been an adjustment being here." He needed to be careful about what he said. The McCrays knew nothing of Henrietta's stipulation that he had to stay. As far as they knew, he was here because he wanted to be. "It's been fun getting to know everyone."

"How long are you planning on staying? You have a brother, too, correct?" Sam asked.

Out of the corner of his eye, Quinn sat up straighter, and he could swear she moved closer to him.

"I'll be headed back to Houston at the end of the holidays."

Quinn sagged into her seat.

"Really? I'm surprised. Are you planning on coming back?" Helen rose and refilled her coffee.

Ash didn't know what to say to that. He was sure there would be more trips to Elf Hollow, but the plan wasn't to stay any longer than need be.

He squirmed under the weight of Quinn's stare. "I'm sure we'll return to get things in order."

"You could always leave the running of the business to me. As I've been doing for the last two years." Quinn's voice was sharp, and ice dripped from each word.

"Oh, but you'd miss out on the joy of running it together. Emerson and Henri were happy working side-by-side," Helen said.

Quinn held his gaze for a long moment. A swirl of emotions played over her expression. So many he couldn't distinguish one from another. She finally turned to Helen. "That's a sweet thought, Helen. But it's not like that here. Ash and his brother both have a life back in Houston. They will never be committed to Fisherman's Cottage like Henri and Emerson were."

"That's too bad. Maybe they will bring their families up to visit every year." Sam rose and reached for his wife's hand. "Okay, my dear, we have some last-minute shopping to do." He turned to Ash. "Our daughter and her family will be arriving Christmas Day. I don't want to get caught without gifts for the kids when they get here."

Quinn and Ash were silent as the couple left the room.

Ash reached for her hand under the table, and she didn't pull away. But she didn't curl her fingers in response. Maybe she was having second thoughts about last night. "I missed you," he offered.

"I missed you, too." Her words seemed sincere, but they lacked luster.

"I —"

"I —" They both started at once.

She shook her head and pulled her hand from his. "You go ahead."

"I feel like we need to talk. About last night and what Helen and Sam were talking about," Ash said.

"What's there to talk about? Is there more I need to know?" There was an expectancy in her gaze. For what, he didn't know.

"They caught me off guard. About staying here. I didn't have an answer ready."

"What about now?"

"Don't do this, Quinn."

"Do what, Ash? Make you admit you might feel something for this place, the people? Make you face the fact that it's not always about you?"

"You have no idea what you're talking about. I came here thinking Eric, and I inherited a *place*. Sell it, make some money, start fresh... now..." he ran a hand through his hair and breathed a heavy sigh.

"Now, what?"

"Nothing here changes, Quinn. I don't belong in Elf Hollow. I'm restless, I'd suffocate here." Three weeks ago, there would have been no question. Everything had changed, too fast, and he didn't know where he fit anymore.

She stood up with enough force the chair tipped. "I have things to do to get ready for this afternoon." She stared over his shoulder, her mouth set in anger. "The party starts at seven. What time do Eric and his family arrive? I need to make sure Kylee has their room ready."

"They got into Minneapolis late last night. They'll be here around noon."

"Fine. Everything will be ready. I imagine the diner will need you as they provide all the food." She stormed from the dining room, not waiting for him to answer.

"Quinn, wait—" but she was gone. Probably for the best. He didn't know what he would say.

Chapter Twenty-Seven

Quinn attached the lid to the second crockpot and put up the seal. The second batch of hot cider was done and would stay warm.

Now she needed to start the hot cocoa. She'd been hiding in the kitchen for the last hour, avoiding Eric and his family. They arrived right at noon, as Ash predicted, and she sent them down to the diner for lunch and to find Ash.

She couldn't deal with Eric or Ash right now. The sight of them made her too angry,

She slammed the container holding the shaved chocolate Simon sent over that morning. They shaved all their own dark chocolate for the hot cocoa, all she had to do was put it all together and melt it down. Something she'd never been able to do before because of the gas stove. Thanks to Ash, she'd been working through that fear.

A pang tightened her chest. No, she wasn't going to think about him. Not today. She'd figure it out later, but today was about Henri. Henri and Emerson.

"Hello. Are you in here, Quinn?" Lizzy Larsen came through the door into the room. "There you are. I hope you don't mind. The kids and I walked back from the diner. They've never seen this much snow. They were itching to get out and play."

Oxygen fled Quinn's brain, and she cringed. "No. That's fine. Can I get you something?" She scrubbed her palms down the front of the apron, painfully aware of the layer of powdered sugar that coated the front. The sloppy bun, secured to the top of her head and her au natural makeup combined to make frumpy look good. What she needed was confidence.

Lizzy was everything Quinn imagined when she thought of wealthy, big city life.

Not a blond hair out of place. Makeup, perfectly there-not there except for the soft coral of her lips. Not a wrinkle on her clothes, despite the four-hour drive from the cities. The only thing that stood out as unexpected were her nails. Long and manicured with Christmas red polish, four boasted a whimsical painted Santa suit.

"The kids are out back with another group of kids. I thought I would come see if I can help you."

"I appreciate that. But, you're a guest. I'm sure you want to get settled..." Her voice trailed into oblivion as the intruder roamed the kitchen.

Lizzy headed toward the pantry. "Is this where you keep the aprons?" She swung the door open, oohed at her discovery, and took one off the hook. As she slid it over her head, she crossed the floor. "What can I do first?"

"Huh... There really isn't much to do here, Lizzy. Ash and the crew at the diner will make most of the food for tonight. I've got the drinks, a few cold dips to put together—"

"Great, while you make the cocoa, I'll put together one of the dips. Point me to the recipe, and I'll get started."

"Sure. Okay." Quinn gritted her teeth. All Larsens were on her hit list right now. And whether by blood or by name, this woman was a Larsen. One of the last people she wanted to deal with. But Minnesota nice won out. She put all the ingredients on the table and handed the woman Henri's recipe for onion dip.

Back at the stove, she stood as far as she could and still stir the pot. Why was the woman in her kitchen? Think, Quinn. She's a guest. You've always been able to talk to guests, Lizzy was no different. "Did you have a nice drive up this morning?"

"We did. It's beautiful here. I've lived in Houston all my life. Except for the occasional trip, I haven't seen this much snow either. I think I was as excited as the kids." She giggled.

Quinn didn't want to like the woman, but her genuine nature was infectious. "The cold can be overwhelming if you're not used to it."

"I can see that. Eric said Ash has had a difficult time adjusting to the cold. But that doesn't surprise me."

Quinn shuffled from one foot to the other. The idea that this woman could be a fountain of information flitted through her thoughts. Maybe she could pick her brain a bit. "Why doesn't it surprise you?"

"Ash doesn't do well with change. I've always thought of him as more of a hothouse animal." Lizzy mixed together the sour cream and the spices. "Do you have a container you want me to put this in?"

"The cabinet behind you. I think Ash has adapted pretty well. After we got him set up in the right gear."

"Hmmm. I guess, but I'm sure he can't wait to get home. How about you? How are you going to feel about the warmer weather?"

The hot chocolate melted, Quinn took a ladle and scooped it into another crockpot to keep warm. "What do you mean?"

"After you're married. We have three temperatures in Houston, hot, super hot, and melt your tires on the road hot."

The ladle clattered out of Quinn's hand, chocolate splattered everywhere. She turned a blank stare at the other woman. "Married?"

"Oh no. I'm sorry. I must have ruined the surprise." Lizzy wiped her hands on her apron and ran a dishcloth underwater. Wringing it out, she approached Quinn and started dabbing at the mess. "When I overheard Eric on the phone with Ash the other night, I assumed he'd already asked you. I bet he's going to ask you tonight. Me and my big mouth..."

Lizzy's voice droned on in the background, white noise in Quinn's head. Marriage? Ash was going to ask her to marry him? Her heart sank. Then it was true. It had all been a ruse.

All lies.

Vertigo swirled in her head. Nausea curdled her stomach and threatened to toss lunch all over the front of the faultless woman now standing in the middle of Quinn's nightmare. She tried to push Lizzy's hands away, but the weightlessness that consumed her made it difficult to move.

Her brain tried to make excuses for him. Maybe he really did want to marry her. Loved her. But she couldn't get past the words in Sadie's letter. If he married, he'd finally claim his trust fund. He expected her to move to Houston. What did he think would happen to Fisherman's Cottage? The diner and shop? Elf Hollow.

It was a trick. He'd laid down a challenge that day in the attorney's office, and she'd been naive enough to think she'd persuade *him*. Show him the beauty of this place. Instead, she'd fallen under his spell.

He and Eric would sell their share to whoever would buy it, and she'd be left to mend another broken heart and battle her new partners.

When would she learn?

❄

Ash led Eric out the door of the diner after making sure everything was ready for tonight. He left Simon with instructions to finish a couple of dishes.

The breakfast conversation with Quinn stuck in his head. She'd wanted something from him. Something he hadn't been ready to give. If he married her, accepted his trust fund, what did that make him?

A monster.

Quinn wasn't leaving Elf Hollow. Married or not. This was her home, and she would fight for it. Just one of the reasons he loved her.

Would that be enough?

"You've been very quiet all morning. What's going through that deep head of yours?" Eric's voice penetrated the fog. "And don't tell me nothing. I'm tired of that answer."

Ash's steps slowed. "No matter what I do... no matter what choice I make... Quinn gets hurt. And I never wanted that to happen."

"How? If you love her, marry her. That's what I've been trying to get through that thick skull of yours."

"She's not going to leave here."

"Why not? If she loves you, she'll leave."

"And when she finds out about the trust fund?"

Eric shook his head.

"See, even you don't have the answer to that one." His grandmother might have intended to help, but the strings she attached to him did nothing but tangle him in a web of heartache. "I can't marry. Not now." Maybe never. She may never forgive him. And his heart was no longer his own.

They walked the last block in silence and entered the house. He tossed his coat on a chair and led the way to the kitchen. "Quinn's probably in the kitchen getting ready."

Ash swung through the door and was greeted by two solemn faces.

Eric slid in past him to his wife and kissed her on the cheek. "What have you two been doing?"

Lizzy cocked her head and ignoring her husband, mouthed *I'm sorry* at Ash. "Getting to know each other. I thought since she was going to be my sister-in-law—"

"What?" Both men shouted at the same time.

"— We should spend some time together."

"What did you say to her, Lizzy? Quinn, are you okay?" Her face was whiter than the powder sugar that coated her hair and the counter.

"Why did your sister-in-law think we were getting married?"

"I don't know. I never said that. Exactly."

"But you must have said something to make her think that. Right?"

"I overheard a conversation between Eric and Ash, I assumed he'd asked you. All this is my fault. Ask Eric, I'm terrible about presuming and putting my nose where it doesn't belong. And it soooo doesn't belong here." The misery on her face would have made him sympathetic if she hadn't opened an entire case of worms on him.

One glance at Quinn and his heart revved like a Nascar engine. He took a step toward her. "Quinn, I can explain."

"No. Don't come near me." She held her hand up between them. "When were you planning on telling me about your grandmother's will?"

"Her will?" First confusion, then understanding.

"One of the letters from Sadie. She told Henri about the trust fund. You have to find someone and settle down and marry to claim that money. I bet it's a lot, isn't it?"

He couldn't speak. The hurt on her face was too much to take in.

At his silence, she continued. "And what was the plan? Mmm? Get me to fall in love with you, marry me, collect your

217

trust fund. Then I would be ecstatic and agree to leave everyone here in a lurch and trip off after you to Texas? Did you really think I was that fickle? I would drop everything I hold dear for a man? Then again, I suppose you would think everyone would stoop to your level."

Her words knifed a hole through his heart. Not that he blamed her for them. "That's not how it is."

"Really? Can you look me in the eye and tell me I'm wrong?" Her eyes pleaded.

"Okay, I think we're all getting carried away here."

"Shut-up, Eric." Both Ash and Quinn shouted at the same time.

"Quinn, I love you..."

"All I want to hear from you Ash is, this isn't some elaborate scheme. But you can't. Because I know everything, and you didn't tell me." Her bottom lip trembled as she pulled the apron over her head. "I can't believe anything you say now."

She grabbed her coat and headed out the backdoor. A sob reached his ears as the door banged shut.

No surprise he'd screwed that up. She'd probably never speak to him again.

"Well, are you going after her, or are you standing here?" Lizzy asked.

"I don't know." His head swung from Eric to Lizzie. "Am I?" He asked her.

"Oh, for goodness sake, yes. Go after her."

Chapter Twenty-Eight

Ash blew on his hands and stamped his feet. In a rush to catch up to Quinn before she could lock herself away, he ran out without his coat. After ten minutes of beating on her door with no answer other than Niko's bark, he regretted that decision. He didn't know how much longer he would make it outside this door.

"Come on, Quinn. It's cold. We can't leave it like this. All I'm asking for is five minutes." He took a seat on the chair. He regretted the move the instant the ice melted and soaked into his jeans. Niko scratched and whined at the door. "I know, Buddy. I would like to come in, but your owner is stubborn." He yelled the last word loud enough to make it through the door.

"Go away, Ash. We have nothing more to say."

He jumped up and leaned his head against the door. "We have a lot to say. We can't leave it like this. We deserve more than that."

A long pause followed by a bang. "You're right. We don't deserve this. But I'm not the one that made the choice to be deceitful. You did." Her voice shook over the words as it muffled through the door. The curtain over the window fluttered into place.

"You owe me a chance to explain. I never lied to you."

"I owe you nothing. A lie of omission is still a lie. Go away. I fulfilled my portion of Henrietta's will. I tried to show you everything this place is. What it means to others. You can lead an ass to water, but you can't make them drink."

"I think you mean horse."

"I mean ass."

Ouch. Okay, maybe he deserved that. He tapped his forehead on the door. "Let me in so we can talk about this."

The lock clicked, but the door didn't open. His heart stuttered with a glimmer of hope. He turned the knob, and the door gave way. Blessed heat greeted him as he stepped into the room.

He stood in front of the fire and rubbed his hands over his arms. "Thank you. I was almost a statue." Niko panted at his side, waiting for his attention. He reached down and fluffed the dog's fur. "At least you're happy to see me," he mumbled for Niko's ears only.

"You said you only needed five minutes. Your time is ticking away." She pointed to her watch and glared at him.

"I don't want to leave things like we did —"

"You mean with you admitting you planned to dupe me into marrying you? Why not? Seems to me you stand to gain a lot with that move. Get me to marry you, and you can collect Sadie's trust fund, and then once we're married, of course, I would agree to sell this place."

"Now you're putting words in my mouth. I never admitted any of that."

"Because you *lied*."

He ground his teeth. "Now, you're being unreasonable. I came here to talk, and you're throwing accusations."

She snorted. "If the accusation fits." She pinched the

bridge of her nose and closed her eyes. "What do you want from me, Ash?"

"I meant what I said the other night. I love you, Quinn. That wasn't a lie. I didn't make that up. I love you." He crossed the floor to her in three strides and gripped her upper arms forcing her to look at him.

"What are you going to do about it?"

He jerked back. "What do you mean? I love you. Isn't that enough?"

"No, it's not enough. Ash, you don't know what love is. You've told me how your father treats you. You've admitted you've never gotten close to anyone." She sighed and stepped away from him. "What would someone like you know about love?"

He fell into the couch and dropped his head into his hands. She knew how to go for the jugular. "You're right. I don't know what love is. Other than Eric and Lizzy, I have no idea what a healthy relationship looks like. But I know what I feel for you, Quinn. It's real. I wish I knew how to make you believe."

"How can I trust anything you say to me? All these weeks, you were building a wall of lies."

This time her words drew blood. He didn't blame her, she was right on all counts. He had no right to ask anyone to love him. "Isn't love supposed to be enough?"

She whirled on him. "You love me. Cool. What does that mean?" She glared up at him. "Seriously, what does it mean?"

"Well ... it means I love you. I want to be with you."

"Okay. But what does it *mean*? Come on, Ash. What do those three words mean to *you*?"

He stared at her blankly. His mind reeled with the knowledge he didn't know what she wanted from him.

"What do you want from me, Quinn? I'm trying here. I

never thought I would find someone I could fall for like this. Tell me what you want me to say, and I'll say it."

She crossed her arms and glared a white heat that burned to his core. "Where did you see our lives going? When you picture us riding off into the sunset together, where are we headed, Ash? Are we here? Running the business, we both inherited. Or are we in Houston, where I follow along with whatever whim you have for the moment?"

That stopped him. "I thought we would eventually end up in Houston."

"I knew it! You are low. You figured I would be so quick to follow after you that I would abandon everything I hold dear."

"Isn't that what married couples do?"

"Yes. When the love is pure and real and natural. Not the ugly thing you made it to be."

"But don't you see. We could start something of our own. Like Henri and Emerson did. Start fresh, build a restaurant of our own."

"You don't get it. I have all that right here." She buried her face in her hands and shook her head. Then dropped them at her side. "Please leave, Ash."

"But—"

"Get. Out." Fresh tears raked across her cheeks, and she hung her head.

"You told me you loved me the other night. I'll leave when you tell me you don't."

She pinned him with a solid glare. "I don't love you, Ash. I never did. Because the man I fell in love with doesn't exist. Now, get out." Her voice never wavered. Her gaze was intense and convincing.

He drank her in. The image needed to last him a lifetime. "I'm sorry."

The walk back to the house was lost on him. He felt nothing, saw nothing. He snuck in the kitchen and worked his way up the back stairs to his room. Thankfully Eric and Lizzy were no longer around. He didn't think he could face either of them right now.

It was better this way. He was toxic. Quinn was right to doubt him when he didn't even know what he wanted.

He'd spent his life building a defense to justify his behavior. He never stopped to question why, as an adult, he still clung to old hurts.

His heart knew he loved her. But his love was never pure. Not like she deserved.

His father had been right all along. He was worthless.

He threw his suitcase on the bed and started tossing in his clothes. He needed to leave.

Chapter Twenty-Nine

Quinn plastered a smile on her face and greeted her guests as they came down the stairs to join the party and the employees and their families as they arrived.

This was it. Everything they'd planned for all month came down to tonight and tomorrow. The reason people came to Elf Hollow year after year was to celebrate Christmas, and it was her first year on her own. "I hope I don't let you down, Henri. I tried to convince Eric and Ash not to sell, but I failed you. Hopefully, the party will be a huge success."

Jim Lovette and his wife and kids were off in the corner, talking to Carole Ann and her husband. Amy, with her current stray, entertained the diner employees over by the drink table. The McCrays were sitting court on the couch by the fireplace with some of the other guests. Children fluttered everywhere. Christmas music and murmured voices filled the house, and the food table sagged under the weight of all the goodies available. Everything was perfect. Exactly as they'd planned.

She caught Jim's eye across the room, and he nodded at

her before he excused himself from his group and made his way over to her.

"Everyone's here. Time to get the party started." The reindeer tie he'd worn for years, with its red bulb, blinked cheerfully. Darkness crossed his face. "What's wrong? Do you need to sit down?"

She blew out a slow, gentle breath, begging the hummingbird wings that drummed in her ears to stop long enough for her to think. "I'm fine. Nerves. This is my first time opening the party." Never mind it might also be her last.

She grabbed a champagne glass off the table and headed to the stairs, climbing to the fourth one from the bottom. The same place Henri stood year after year, Emerson by her side until the last two. With a shaky hand, she gripped the smooth, wooden rail holding herself upright and waited.

Jim turned off the music and called for everyone's attention. Every eye in the house turned to her, right down to the youngest child.

A jagged ball of fear stuck her tongue to the roof of her mouth. "I want to welcome..." Her voice cracked, she rubbed fingers down her throat and tried again. "I guess I'm a bit nervous. It doesn't feel right taking the Wagners' place up here. I keep expecting Henri to barrel out the kitchen door any minute, bellowing orders."

Everyone laughed at the memory.

"I think this was their favorite day of the year. When everyone was gone, and the guests all tucked in bed, they'd sit over there by the fire, and rehash the entire month. Laughing and enjoying all the stories while they were still fresh. The joy they brought to all of us on this night was nothing compared to the joy you gave them. And every year, they'd kiss me goodnight with the promise of next year." *I. Will. Not. Cry.* But moisture blurred her vision anyway.

"All our employees and their families meant so much to

them and me. Thank you for all you do throughout the year to make this a special place. To our guests, without you, we wouldn't be standing here today. We thank you for your repeated visits and your willingness to share your families with us year after year." She swallowed. "This is our first year without Henri. Our third without Emerson. Their absence fills the room as much as their presence ever did. Whatever happens in the future, we will always hold them in our memories and their legacy in our hearts." She raised her glass. "To Henri and Emerson. Merry Christmas." *And happy birthday, Henri. You, to Sadie.*

"Merry Christmas," everyone shouted in unison and raised their glasses of champagne or alcohol-free grape juice, and toasted. And then the music was turned back on, and the conversation flowed again.

"Quinn, come see me." Carole Ann motioned for her and patted the spot next to her on the double chair in the parlor.

Quinn grinned and sat next to her. "I see all your chicks are home for the holidays and here to celebrate with you. How did you manage that?"

Carole Ann's kids had been coming to the celebration as long as Quinn could remember. Her two oldest had kids themselves running around with the others. Her heart swelled. Her family.

She pushed the worry from her head. No need to borrow trouble. It would show up soon enough. "I'm surprised your hubby let you come."

"Are you kidding, wild horses couldn't me keep from this. We all look forward to this every year." She wrapped an arm around Quinn and pulled her into a hug. "Besides, I wanted to be here to support you. Hubs and the boys maneuvered me to this chair, and here I sit. The grandkids are my runners. If I try to walk, I'll be sent home."

"I'm glad you're here. I've missed seeing you every day."

"I know. But..." her voice trailed off.

"But what?"

"It's been nice being home."

"You're not bored yet?"

A secretive smile lit the older woman's face. "Sitting still, yes. But I've enjoyed the time with my family. Where's Ash? I haven't seen him. I met Eric and his family. Oh, no. What happened, sweetie?"

Quinn swiped the tears before they could spill over. "It was all a lie, Carole Ann."

"What was the lie?"

"Ash. Everything. He and Eric never intended to keep the properties."

"But, you knew that."

"Yes, but... I thought I could change his, *their* mind. And I couldn't."

Carole Ann tucked a strand of Quinn's hair behind her ear and cupped her face. "What was the lie?"

Quinn's lips thinned. "I... I..." she stammered. "I found a letter. From Sadie, she tied Ash's inheritance into a trust fund that he can't access until he gets married."

"He asked you to marry him?"

"No. But he said he loved me."

"Hmm."

"What? What does *hmmm* mean?" Quinn asked.

"I'm thinking. When he declared his love for you, did he tell you he was going to sell his share of Henri's estate?"

Quinn crossed her arms and glanced away. She didn't like where this was headed. "No."

"So, I ask again, what was the lie?"

There'd been a lie. She was sure of it. It was in there somewhere, buried. But for the life of her, she couldn't find it now.

Chapter Thirty

A sh tossed the remote on the bed and roamed the dark hotel room. Nothing but silly cheerful holiday movies about redemptions and second chances. Families and happy endings.

He'd arrived in Minneapolis after midnight the night before. Thanks to yet another snowfall, he'd been delayed three hours.

Nerves shattered after the treacherous drive, he'd checked-in to the room and prepared to wait for his flight out of town in forty-eight hours. As exhausted as he was, sleep wouldn't give him the release he craved. Elf Hollow and images of Quinn invaded his every waking moment.

About now, Christmas morning gift exchange and breakfast were over, and the folks at Fisherman's Cottage sat around enjoying time with family and friends. He experienced a momentary pang of guilt as he thought of the dinner prep ahead. He should be there. It was his job.

She wouldn't welcome him. Quinn was happier with him gone. He needed to remind himself of that. Hopefully, Simon or Barney came to help. If not, they'd prepared all of the dishes ahead of time. All she would need to do is reheat.

A decision needed to be made. With sudden clarity, he realized Quinn was the only thing he needed, wanted, from Elf Hollow. But Quinn wouldn't be Quinn *without* Elf Hollow. It was time to talk to Eric. He pulled his phone from his coat pocket, where he put it after turning it off. He waited for it to power up, his body heavy.

Fifteen missed calls and seven text messages. His heart skipped, and he scrolled through the screen in the hope at least one of them was from Quinn. But all of the text messages were from Eric demanding to know what was going on.

Except one. Phil, their investigator, left him a message the day before telling him to listen to his voicemail. He'd been trying to reach him all day. He flipped through all the messages, all Eric until he got to Phil's.

"Hey man, I've been trying to reach you. I have the information you wanted on Emerson Wagner. Emerson Wagner is listed on Sam McAllister's birth certificate. Sam McAllister is your Quinn's father. Her grandmother, Patricia, and Wagner went to the University of Minnesota at the same time. I tracked down a friend of Patricia's who filled in some of the blanks. I'll email it all to you, but in a nutshell, Emerson and Patricia come from different worlds. She left school when she found out she was pregnant. Her friend said Patricia told everyone, including her son, the father was dead. Child Protective Services must've tracked Emerson through the birth certificate when Quinn's folks died."

Ash hung up. Pondering the information. Quinn was Emerson's granddaughter. Why did they hide that from her?

Maybe Emerson was too ashamed. Didn't want to face Quinn's potential rejection of him. How sad for the man that he never claimed her as his.

He scanned his surroundings. Same room different city.

Lifeless. Generic. His mind wandered again to Elf Hollow. How ironic and pathetic that he finally found a woman that made him happy. That he could, as Eric said, come home to every night. And he'd lost her over that stupid trust fund.

He wasn't sure what he would do now. His life was no longer in Houston. He didn't know where it was. All he knew was he loved Quinn.

He kept replaying her question. What do those words mean? Her gaze pleaded for him to get it. Nothing else mattered, but Quinn. What else did she want from him?

He sat up straighter. None of it mattered. The money, the restaurant, the inheritance ... it was all a distraction. Something to help forget he was alone in the world. But he didn't have to be alone anymore. Quinn loved him. What else could a man need?

His heart pounded as he reached for his phone. Now that the idea took hold, he couldn't let it go. Couldn't wait.

Their company kept an attorney on retainer. Technically he wasn't an employee anymore, but the attorney had always been decent to him. Maybe he would overlook that one fact. He searched for the man's number in his contacts and placed the call. The man picked up after the third ring.

"Hello, Raymond? This is Ash Larson. I'm sorry to bother you on Christmas Day, but I need some information."

Chapter Thirty-One

E veryone turned as a cold blast of air preceded Ash through the door of Fisherman's cottage four hours later.

"Ash, what are you doing here?" Quinn's voice rose in shock.

Everyone sat around the living room, after dinner coffees in hand. Niko barked and raced across the room to greet him. At least the dog missed him.

"Quinn, I need to talk to you. It's important."

They all turned to Quinn and held their collective breath.

Her lips parted, and she nodded.

In addition to the guests, all her managers and their families were here. Eric and Lizzy relaxed and easily fit into this group.

Quinn approached him. "Do you want to go to my office?"

"No. I need to say this here. I want witnesses for this. I'm not sure how to say it, so I'm just going to put it out there. You're Emerson Wagner's granddaughter."

"What?" She shoved a hand over her mouth.

The room gasped and murmured words floated around. "I see that now. That makes perfect sense."

"Is that true?"

"It is. I found something in one of my grandmother's letters, and I had our investigator check into it. Emerson and your grandmother met at the University of Minnesota. She left when she found out she was pregnant with your father because she didn't think Emerson's family would accept her. She never told anyone. Including Emerson. I'm guessing he found out when..."

A wild expression clouded her face.

"When Child Protective Services contacted the Wagners," he finished.

"But how did they know? My father said his dad died in a car crash before he was born."

"That's what your grandmother told everyone. But the birth certificate lists Emerson as the father."

Quinn dropped onto the arm of the chair where Amy sat. "Why wouldn't he tell me? Why keep this secret?" Her voice shook, and her hand scrubbed across her forehead.

"I don't know. Maybe he was ashamed to tell you. Henri gave us those letters for a reason. There were answers in them she wanted us to have."

"I wish he'd told me."

"Emerson was a proud man." Carole Ann said. "I think Ash is right, I think he was too ashamed, all he could do was give you love."

"My mom always said Emerson attached to you instantly," Amy added. "You were his shadow."

"I remember. They were both wonderful when I arrived. But he went out of his way to make me feel... *accepted*."

Ash waited. Gave her time to process the new information.

She rose and wrapped her arms around him. "Thank you."

Her heat branded him. The scent of rain filled him. He encircled her in his arms, determined to take it all in, in case she kicked him to the curb after the next thing he had to say. "It's a lot to process."

"That's an understatement."

"There's more."

"More? Secrets?"

"More revelations. Would you rather wait?" *Please don't wait.* "I understand. If you need time."

"Might as well get it all over with. Lay it on me."

"Here?"

She cocked her head and chewed her lower lip. "Why not here? It seems my life is suddenly an open book. Might as well keep going with the story."

He hadn't expected an audience for this part, but if that's the way she wanted it. "I get it now, Quinn. What you were asking me last night in your cottage. I know what those words mean to me now. I. Love. You. No matter what. No matter where we live. No matter how you feel in return. Rich or poor. I love you. Nothing else is as important as you, Quinn McAllister. Without you, I can't be the man I'm meant to be. The me that I am with you, doesn't exist outside of us."

"Ash—"

He put his finger to his mouth. "Shhh. I'm not done." He handed her a sealed envelope. "In there is a note that I wrote per my attorney's direction. It directs the trustee of my grandmother's estate to disperse my trust fund to her favorite charity."

"Ash, you can't be serious?" Eric said.

"Sit down. Be quiet, Eric." Lizzy stopped him with a hand on his arm.

The muscles in Ash's face relaxed and stretched into a smile. "Without her, the money doesn't matter. My life is here with you, Quinn. If you'll have me." He held his breath. Waited for her to say something. Anything.

Quinn's gaze darted around the room. To all the familiar faces, to the envelope in her hand.

He held his hands up to stop anything she might have said. "You don't have to say anything right away. I'm gonna go." His mouth opened and closed, and he pointed to the door. This had been a stupid idea. He should never have come here. It was too much at once. "Oh, there's another letter in there was well. Turning over my share of Fisherman's Cottage and the rest of it to you. I... Merry Christmas, everyone."

He left before embarrassment and loss could sink its fangs any further into his heart. He accomplished what he set out to do. Laid it all bare. That's all that mattered.

Quinn's lungs choked off all air, and her hands trembled. Why was he leaving? He dropped two huge bombshells and then leaves? "Ash. Wait." But he was gone. Door closed. "Excuse me." She chased him out the door.

He was halfway to the car when she hit the porch. "You think you can come in here, spread all this Christmas cheer and then run? Think again, Cowboy."

"I wanted to give you time to take it all in."

A shiver ripped through her, and she huffed into her cupped hands as she took the steps to meet him on the icy path. "I've taken it in. But you left before you gave me a chance to say anything."

"Okay, let's go back inside before you freeze to death. You can tell me there."

"Why would you do that? Walk away from your trust fund? Aren't you going to miss it?"

He crammed his hands into his pockets and rocked back

and forth on his heels. "It cost me nothing to let go of something I never had. But, to walk away from Elf Hollow, Niko... *you*... would cost me everything."

Like a cloud, his words floated beneath her, launching her feet off the ground. A thrill shot from her chest outward. He was willing to give it all up. For her. Who else would do that?

She swiped a tear. "I've guarded my heart for a while now. Pretending I didn't need anything but this place. I'm told that's what Henri was afraid I'd do. I also found out recently that she and Emerson were quite the matchmakers. They had a knack for putting people together." In her heart, she suspected throwing the two of them together was Henri's last match.

"You're loyal to everyone here. They're lucky to have you on their side."

"Somehow you, Ash Larsen, got under my skin. Showed me there is more to life than burying my head in the snowbanks. I love you. And I want you here. I want us to make our mark on Henri and Emerson's legacy. But I can't do that with me here and you wherever you're going to be." She shivered.

He moved closer, rubbed his hands up and down her arms.

Joy exploded like confetti from New Year's Eve balloons at his touch. Their gazes tangled across the breath of space.

"Be sure of what you're saying, Quinn. I'm ready to walk away if that will make you happy, but I don't think I can get my hopes up only to have them dashed."

"Carole Ann told me at dinner she's been enjoying this time with her family, and she's not planning on coming back after her release. The diner is going to need a new head chef. And I think we can make some improvements there. My mind has been swimming with ideas." She stopped and traced the outline of his firm bottom lip with the pad of her thumb. "Know anyone looking for a job?"

The expression on his face glowed. His tense body relaxed. "Well, darlin', I might know someone. He's dirt poor, so he doesn't come cheap. And he puts his booted foot in his mouth from time to time."

"I think we can work with that." She lifted to her toes, cupped the back of his head. Her lips trailed across his jawline to his mouth, peppered his face, until she pressed her lips against his. His response pushed all else from her mind as he hit her with a searing kiss that steamed the air around them.

He took control of the kiss, cradling her head in his hands.

As they pulled apart, he trailed three kisses across her cheek. "I love you, Quinn McAllister, and I'll spend the rest of my life making sure you never doubt that."

The Christmas moon shone behind him. The glow of the Aurora Borealis floated with greens and blues in the night sky.

"I'm going to hold you to that. I love you. Merry Christmas, Ash."

I hope you enjoyed reading Ash and Quinn's story! Guess what?

You're invite to Elf Hollow's first wedding! Quinn and Ash would love to see you. Follow the link below to get your exclusive bonus scene. And who knows? You might just catch a glimpse of the next Christmas couple!

https://dl.bookfunnel.com/5b9yl28s9i

Where to find me

Enjoy this book? You can make a big difference.

Reviews are the most powerful tools in my writing arsenal when it comes to getting attention for my books. Much as I'd like to, I don't have the financial muscle of a New York publisher. I can't take out full page ads or join every ad platform.

(Not yet! Just wait!)

But I do have something much more powerful and effective than that, and it's something those publishers would kill to get their hands on.

A committed and loyal bunch of readers!

Honest reviews of my books help bring them to the attention of other readers.

If you've enjoyed this book I would be grateful if you would spend just a few minutes to leave a review (It can be as short as you'd like) on the book's Amazon page. You can jump right to the page by clicking the link below.

Review

Thank you bunches!!
    Savannah

Visit Savannah Ford
    Website:https://www.savannahfordauthor.com

Goodreads:https://www.goodreads.com/author/show/19768993.Savannah_Ford

Facebook:https://www.facebook.com/Savannahfordauthor

Also by Savannah Ford

It Happened One Winter by Savannah Ford

Love at The Bluebonnet Inn by Savannah Ford

Love, Lattes, and Lonely Hearts by Savannah Ford

Other books in the Elf Hollow series: by Daphne Dyer

Restaurant Wars author Daphne Dyer

The Puppy Bribe author Daphne

Coming in March 2023 Sweet Autumn Kisses author Savannah Ford

Cardinal Point series:

When Love Leads You Home

The Father-Daughter Picnic

A Promise for Tomorrow

My Half-Price Valentine

A Blessing of the Heart

Almost Home for the Holidays

The Widow's Christmas Ruse

It Happened One Winter by Savannah Ford

Red, White and Baby Blue

Love at The Bluebonnet Inn by Savannah Ford

Love, Lattes, and Lonely Hearts by Savannah Ford

You can follow Cardinal Point on Facebook.

About the Author

Savannah Ford writes sweet contemporary romances with just a dash of heat to bring you swoon-worthy kisses that lead to happily ever afters.

She lives in the frozen tundra of Minnesota after living in balmy Houston for many years. She loves cozying down in front of a roaring fire, a mug of frothy cocoa, and happily-ever-after Hallmark movies, especially the Christmas kind. When she's not writing, reading, or spending time with her family, she's in her studio where she builds dollhouses.

Savannah lives with the hero of her own story, two kids, a singing bloodhound named Elvis, and one-year-old Hailey the Labradoodle

If you enjoy an edgier read, she writes romantic suspense under her pen name, Kimberly Ford.

https://www.savannahfordauthor.com

Also by Kimberly Ford

And, if you liked this book consider my romantic suspense line written under Kimberly Ford. If you like a little suspense with a little more grit, head on over to Amazon and pick up Searching For Eden, my debut novel.

Made in the USA
Middletown, DE
08 March 2024

51085687R00149